MW00623013

THE REST IS SILENCE

AUGUSTO MONTERROSO (1921–2003) was born in Tecuigalpa, Honduras, to a Honduran mother and a Guatemalan father, who founded several newspapers. Shuttled between his parents' two countries throughout his childhood, Monterroso never finished grammar school. As a teenager in Guatemala he worked as a cashier in a butcher's shop and read voraciously, cofounding a literary society and the intellectual journal *Acento*, which opposed the dictatorship of President Jorge Ubico. After Ubico's successor had him imprisoned in 1944, Monterroso managed to escape and was granted political asylum in Mexico. He briefly served as a Guatemalan diplomat in Bolivia and spent two years in Chile before returning to Mexico, where he remained for the rest of his life, working as a professor and an editor. He was the author of several highly regarded books of stories (including *Complete Works and Other Stories*, *The Black Sheep and Other Fables*, and *Perpetual Motion*), essays, fictionalized memoirs (*The Gold Seekers* and *La Vaca*), and the novel *The Rest Is Silence*. He was awarded the Juan Rulfo Prize for Latin American and Caribbean Literature, among other honors.

AARON KERNER has worked as an editor for Dalkey Archive Press and David R. Godine, Publisher / Black Sparrow Books and has translated, most recently, Benedetta Craveri's *The Last Libertines*. He teaches literature and film at the Commonwealth School in Boston, Massachusetts.

DUSTIN ILLINGWORTH is a writer who lives in Northern California. His work has appeared in *The New York Review of Books*, *The New Yorker*, and *The New York Times Book Review*.

THE REST IS SILENCE
The Life and Works of Eduardo Torres

AUGUSTO MONTERROSO

Translated from the Spanish by
AARON KERNER

Introduction by
DUSTIN ILLINGWORTH

NEW YORK REVIEW BOOKS

New York

THIS IS A NEW YORK REVIEW BOOK
PUBLISHED BY THE NEW YORK REVIEW OF BOOKS
207 East 32nd Street, New York, NY 10016
www.nyrb.com

This translation is supported in part by a grant from Acción Cultural Española.

AC/E
ACCIÓN CULTURAL
ESPAÑOLA

Library of Congress Cataloging-in-Publication Data
Names: Monterroso, Augusto, author. | Kerner, Aaron, translator.
Title: The rest is silence / by Augusto Monterroso; translated by Aaron Kerner.
Other titles: Lo demás es silencio. English
Description: New York: New York Review Books, 2024. | Series: New York
  Review Books classics
Identifiers: LCCN 2024006485 (print) | LCCN 2024006486 (ebook) |
  ISBN 9781681378824 (paperback) | ISBN 9781681378831 (ebook)
Subjects: LCGFT: Novels.
Classification: LCC PQ7297.M62 L613 2024 (print) | LCC PQ7297.M62
  (ebook) | DDC 863/.64—dc23/eng/20240215
LC record available at https://lccn.loc.gov/2024006485
LC ebook record available at https://lccn.loc.gov/2024006486

ISBN 978-1-68137-882-4
Available as an electronic book; ISBN 978-1-68137-883-1

Printed in the United States of America on acid-free paper.
10 9 8 7 6 5 4 3 2 1

CONTENTS

PART III: APHORISMS, MAXIMS, ETC.

PART IV: IMPROMPTU COLLABORATIONS

ADDENDUM

INTRODUCTION

AUGUSTO Monterroso's *The Rest Is Silence*, a fictional Festschrift for a provincial Mexican intellectual, teems with invented texts, imaginary writers, dubious footnotes, possible pseudonyms, and unreliable memories. The novel's constituent parts reveal the social, cultural, and literary life of one Eduardo Torres, a writer and elder statesman of the fictional town of San Blas, Mexico. Its four sections—grouped loosely into tributes, selected writings, aphorisms, and "impromptu collaborations"—make a case for compilation as a natural handmaiden to farce. The opening remarks from friends and family are largely hatchet jobs born of petty jealousy or long acquaintance. The selections from Torres's oeuvre—incredible misreadings, all—are bathetic, anodyne, lacking in sense, and almost invariably wrong. Yet the vivisection is marked by compassion as much as it is by savagery. Ferried by the risible figure of Torres, avatar of vanity and misjudgment, Monterroso smuggles a pocket autobiography within his deflation of Mexico's literati. In the process, he forges one of the sublime fools of literature, a man whose commitment to delusion is itself a kind of glorious art.

Augusto Monterroso was born in 1921 in Tecuigalpa, Honduras, to a Guatemalan father and a Honduran mother. He was largely self-taught, his schooling interrupted by frequent migrations between his parents' home countries. While working odd jobs, he attended night classes at the National Library of Guatemala. He was enamored of the Greek and Roman classics—Virgil, Aesop, Catullus—as well as with Cervantes, Shakespeare, Johnson, Byron, Dante, and Rilke. After founding a literary magazine that was critical of the dictator

Jorge Ubico, he petitioned for and was granted asylum in Mexico, where he'd spend most of his remaining years. Respected by his peers, he published only sparingly, a significant but still somehow ancillary figure of the Latin American Boom. Monterroso's reputation today rests on his extraordinary short stories, unclassifiable microfictions suffused with technical sophistication, paradox, wry humor, and metaphysical irreverence. ("The Dinosaur," perhaps the shortest story in all of literature, reads in its entirety: "When he awoke, the dinosaur was still there.") He died in Mexico City in 2003.

Monterroso siphoned energy from the short story form to fuel what would be his only novel. The "tributes" that open *The Rest Is Silence* are vigorous, combative, funny, flush with character and incident. They are also interconnected and reflexive, a mini-roundelay. Likewise, the fictional essays and reviews possess something of the lacerating energy of Monterroso's *Complete Works* and *Perpetual Motion*, scathing masterpieces of minimalist satire. In its metafictional high jinks, it shares something with Monterroso's contemporary Jorge Luis Borges. One gambit sees Torres reviewing Monterroso's collection *The Black Sheep and Other Fables*. (He calls attention to the author's "paucity of production.") And Torres himself was mentioned in an earlier Monterroso story, "Humor." These porous, portable fictions push against the boundaries of their smallness. They are whetted shards that almost escape the confines of the mosaic.

But Torres's colossal delusion unifies all, an energy field in which the novel's disparate particles constellate. Pompous, self-involved, impractical, and hopelessly fond of his own dithering, he is made ridiculous by the incongruities between his life and his work, his belief and his ability, his spirit and his will, his reputation and his reality. In the unflattering reminiscences of those closest to him, we get a sense of how he spends his days: combing through bookshops for obscure poetry, taking excessively long baths, hanging around younger writers, repeating jokes, basking in local admiration, drinking to excess at parties, and writing much but producing little of any worth. On his origins, his wife is typically laconic: "He became a big deal in San Blas, but that must be because nobody around here knows anything." A self-created man, then, like Monterroso, each wresting an ascension from unlikely circumstances. (San Blas is perhaps not so very far removed from Guatemala City.)

Torres begins his "Writer's Decalogue," a sort of Thirteen Commandments of writing, with the following maxim: "When you have something to say, say it; when you don't, say that as well. Never stop writing." His fidelity to this disastrous precept is almost admirable. Unlike his creator, Torres is calamitously prolific. There is little that escapes his attention. On the past: "One could say that, before History, all was Prehistory." On class struggle: "The Rich should love the Poor and the Poor should love the Rich, for otherwise all is Hate." On contradiction: "If it was not for contradiction, contraries would cease (so to speak) to exist, and, incidentally, to contradict each other." On literary style: "Delete one line per day." On law: "It is strict." Platitudes vie with non sequiturs; absurdities multiply from page to page. One begins to wonder how Torres established his reputation to begin with. Whence the renown, the invitations, the accolades? What spell has he cast over San Blas?

In this case appreciation is perhaps reserved for imaginations already quickened by Torres himself—his presence, his single-mindedness, his allegiance—which is something quite apart from the unfortunate work he produces. Monterroso taught *Don Quixote* at the Universidad Nacional Autónoma de México for many years, and there is something of the mad don about Torres—call it an unwavering fealty to illusion—that ennobles his otherwise ludicrous persona. (Torres's own extraordinary misreading of Cervantes's masterpiece constitutes one of the novel's most hilarious chapters.) Also like Quixote, Torres is a creature of improbable vitality. He has no particular mission, no legible aesthetic, no self-awareness or intellectual rigor. Rather, he possesses a belief in art without which he would cease to exist. With dusty texts and literary supplements, he takes arms against an otherwise disenchanted world.

But only a committed practitioner of such art could so thoroughly lampoon it. Monterroso's mockery is so subtle and convincing because it is always marbled with painful understanding. For Torres, literary criticism is a sacred pursuit. Monterroso's gentle blasphemies, then, suggest the liturgical understanding of the acolyte. His prose—compressed yet supple in Aaron Kerner's fluid translation—is thrillingly ambiguous. Its urbane, ironical sweep offers little room for either exultation or condemnation. Rather, it revels in our inscrutable behaviors, our galling inconsistencies, our lies and evasions, our psychologies stained with fear or failure. "But then tell me," Torres's valet asks, "is there anything having to do with the soul of man that isn't at bottom strange and paradoxical?" This is Monterroso's territory, the hinterlands of human contradiction, where ambivalence and delusion are the sole proofs of a subject's ultimate significance.

The novel closes with an analysis of a poem, "The Burro of San Blas," an impromptu contribution by a pseudonymous critic, or so we're told via footnotes. The piece suggests that the mysterious poem, apparently a minor classic in San Blas, was actually written by Torres. (The poem's implicit attack on Torres himself is thought to be strategic, another shield for his identity.) The analysis is needlessly prolix, rife with parenthetical asides and asinine commentary. It is almost certainly the camouflaged work of Torres himself. There is a dizzying moment—eminently Monterrosan—when we realize we are likely reading Torres on Torres, doubly removed by way of anonymity and pseudonymity, an act whose surpassing indulgence renders it utterly plausible. The poem—terrible by any standard—stages its ambush within a mangled sonnet: "In the town of San Blas, not far away / there dwells a useless ass, they say / Everyone thinks he's exceedingly quick / but nothing of worth ever falls from his lips." The essayist, whoever he or she may be, suggests that Torres is the "only epigrammatist in the history of literature so wholly devoted to self-mockery."

If you squint, this description could extend to the author himself. In his single novel and his many shorter works, Monterroso created a host of composite literary figures whose defects serve as satirical fodder. But it is precisely here, in this motley crew of failed artists and preposterous intellectuals, that Monterroso—aphorist, diarist, elegist, writer of essays and articles and microscopic fictions—reveals his affinity for the ineffectual journeyman, a kind of tender recognition. The consuming obsession, the unfounded arrogance, the despised provincial obscurity, the tireless striving and jealously guarded success: all are ligatures born of familiarity and used to bind these muddled, ridiculous, wonderfully living characters to their creator. They constitute a model of confused passion, one at war with insignificance and resignation, the humiliating undercurrents of literary life. As Torres writes at the novel's end:

> sooner or later, when everything's said and done, all of it will wind up in the trash. If someday somebody takes up that trash once again and from it fabricates a few new sheets of paper, I trust that the next time around said paper will be used for something less ambiguous, less falsely magnanimous, less futile.

Monterroso isn't nearly as trusting. The subtitle of "The Burro of San Blas" more readily suggests his assessment of posterity: "There's Always a Bigger Ass." That may be so. But after spending any time with this wonderfully beguiling novel, one is moved to affirm there will never be another Torres.

—DUSTIN ILLINGWORTH

THE REST IS SILENCE

"The rest is silence."

　　　—SHAKESPEARE, *The Tempest*

EPITAPH[*]

HERE LIES EDUARDO TORRES,
WHO, HIS WHOLE LIFE LONG,
CAME, SAW, AND WAS PERPETUALLY DEFEATED
AS MUCH BY THE ELEMENTS
AS BY THE SHIPS OF THE ENEMY

[*]Father Benito Cereno, the parish priest of San Blas, has deposited the above epitaph for Eduardo Torres in the funerary urn destined to receive its subject. Composed by Torres himself, it will one day be engraved upon his tombstone. Contrary to his wishes, it is being revealed to the public in advance of his death, which event we all hope is still far in the future. Consulted for their opinions, various learned residents of San Blas claim to detect in this epitaph, above and beyond those customary classical allusions so beloved by the maestro, a slightly bitter note, a certain pessimism—inevitable, perhaps, in the face of the vanity of all human effort.

PART I: TRIBUTES

A BRIEF MOMENT IN THE LIFE OF EDUARDO TORRES
*by a Friend**

IT IS ELEVEN fifteen in the morning on one of those summer days so abundant in our corner of the world.

In the depths of the spacious library of the house at no. 208, Calle de Mercaderes, San Blas, S.B., in an uncomfortable leather armchair well-worn by the inexorable passage of time and incessant use, though still in relatively good shape (in keeping with the genteel poverty of its owner), calmly reclines a clearly discomfited gentleman whose age may be safely estimated as somewhere in the neighborhood of fifty-five years, though given his unmistakable fatigue an inattentive observer might perhaps judge him to be rather elderly.

Only an odd tic of obvious psychosomatic origin triggering a contraction of his left cheek every fifteen to twenty seconds—a tic that is, in fact, renowned throughout the city of San Blas thanks to a number of somewhat malevolent witticisms whose origins lie in days gone by, jibes at which their butt, to whom the very idea of malice is foreign, is always the first to laugh—only this tic, which we mentioned several lines earlier, troubles every now and again the serenely pensive expression discernible in that face, which is not merely sallow but also stirred within by, to put it in round numbers, a thousand passions.

From time to time his frigid gaze, incomparably compelling, sheds its steeliness and strays from the volume he is currently perusing to

---

*In reality Juan Islas Mercado, known in San Blas by the nickname "Lord Jim" (a clear literary allusion to the initials of his actual name, which of course the residents of San Blas all understand and celebrate), the former private secretary to Eduardo Torres, who had hoped by means of this pseudonym to preserve his anonymity.

settle after a moment somewhat vaguely, or meditatively, on a yellowing bust of Cicero whose blank eyes survey, in turn, as though across the span of centuries, a recessed wall of bookshelves opposite filled with hardback volumes all delicately bound in calfskin, each of which—as is regularly bruited by the gossip mills of San Blas—the subject of this digression has read at least twice.

For a few brief moments his mind is at rest, and a profoundly bitter rictus surfaces on those lips usually so supple and, if one focuses on their corners, so intensely expressive.

Through the high and broad French windows bursts an agitated mass of sunbeams, five or six of which descend to nest lovingly on the high and somewhat grizzled head of our biographee. The diminutive particles of dust revolving through said light might suggest to an observer—recalling Epicurus—the plurality of worlds. And as if that were not enough, presiding over this singular tableau, and similarly framed by folios of every species, one might contemplate, on the wall opposite the door through which one enters or leaves the room, an enormous portrait in oils of the very subject of these lines, executed by its painter with the selfsame awe that has, in my own case—and as is only appropriate!—commandeered the pen.

Ten minutes later, the expected Commission of Notables of San Blas—comprising two or three intellectuals, a poet, two merchants, and several politicians from various stations of society—makes its surprise appearance precisely at the agreed-upon hour: twelve o'clock noon.

Eduardo Torres (since, to put it plainly, the figure that I will attempt to body forth over the following pages in spite of the poor palette at my disposal is and could be none other than he) receives them, as is his inveterate custom, with circumspect affability, a somewhat pensive solemnity. He embraces them, hailing each by his Christian name (among which, as soon becomes clear, "Pancho" is by no means the least common), and offers each gentleman a seat, directing them now with one hand, now with the other.

Once the elaborate preliminary flourishes appropriate to such an occasion have concluded and the visitors are at rest in their respective chairs, several of them nervously adjusting their collars, Eduardo Torres prepares himself to listen, adopting again that imperturbable yet expectant carriage that has attended him throughout his renowned existence.

And truly, one would expect no less. The emissaries seated before him, representing the state's political movers and shakers, glance sidelong at one another, deeply flustered. The room soon fills with the sound of clearing throats and various other characteristic noises— for instance, the hum of an obstinate fly restlessly circling the bust of the defunct and marmoreal tribune, that intimate (though now sadly mute) witness to the scene.

At that point, Dr. Rivadeneyra, the commission's spokesman (to judge by the discreet but visible nudges with which his companions have striven to spur him to action), declares with much lucid reasoning and rousing praise of Torres's personality, honesty, and wisdom— which attributes are proverbial throughout San Blas—that he intends to request, in the name of the community as a whole, that he, Torres, accept the candidacy for the governorship of this, their more than long-suffering federal entity.

Eduardo Torres listens impassively to his own encomium. Were it not for the aforementioned tic, with which our readers have already been made familiar, one might perhaps have said, to wax metaphorical, that the man had been turned to stone. That swift and well-turned litany of his brilliant attributes—and following on its heels the almost interminable enumeration of the ills that since time immemorial had been visited upon San Blas by the cruelty of its unscrupulous leaders, the continual flooding, and the local bosses who have plunged our poor state over time into anarchy and chaos—leave him unmoved, cognizant as he is (and as who with any experience of the world is not!) that the greatest enemy of the powerful, though it may, like all things weak and deceptive, keep itself concealed, is power itself.

From behind the thick, vaguely grayish curtains where I have concealed myself with pistol in hand, ready to halt in its tracks any unforeseen act of aggression, I observe Eduardo Torres glance (in a very characteristic gesture) upward, as if distracted, at the ceiling while whistling a popular tune, and place the palms of both hands on his thighs; then, applying sufficient force to the latter with the former in order to facilitate this unassuming maneuver, he rises slowly to his feet, whereupon he looks simultaneously and fixedly into the eyes of each of the members of the commission, and, at last, deploying as is his wont the most courteous of excuses—which his audience, having already divined the character of his answer, are prepared to accept with the sort of resignation that only an anticipatory apprehension of the irremediable can bestow—modestly replies that No, his apportioned task is otherwise; that it consists of nothing but the tireless dissemination of ideas, whatever they might be, and wherever they might be found; of defending, as is incumbent upon every good citizen, the land to which fate has personally led him, without, however, imprudently straying from his accustomed foxhole*; of unfalteringly attending to the natural thirst for knowledge that even the humblest man or woman carries into, and indeed out of, this life, without however in any way claiming that said thirst, insatiable though it may be, bestows on its bearer any right or prerogative beyond its simple satisfaction; and he concludes by voicing the suspicion that any position of power such as is being offered to him today would irremediably entail a farrago of responsibilities inimical to the exercise of thought.

"Careful, careful, caballeros!" he firmly concludes, arm raised and index finger trembling feverishly. "Let's not be overhasty here. You know as well as I do that the quickest way to kill an idea is to put it into practice. Leave the book to fulfill those functions natural to it, sans distraction or flattery. If Caesar, with all of his power, should wish to pick up a scrap of papyrus and read it, he'll do so—who can prevent him? My own power, gentlemen, is of course far more modest; and though I see in your generous offer a sort of Palm of Victory over the vices afflicting our state, I warn you that I will not rashly transform myself into an object of my own censure, which, *mutatis mutandis, castigat ridendo mores.*

---

*That is, his desk, journalism.

"There will be others," he continues with a sigh, after a brief pause, "perhaps more fortunate or capable than I, who will be able to transform themselves overnight, like Viriathus, into illustrious generals —latter-day Cincinnatuses or Cocleses. But permit me, I beg you, to pause before that Rubicon reserved historically for the Juliuses of the world and return to my immemorial seclusion, where, far from the world's applause, I shall be better able to serve my happy fellow citizens and to defeat, on my own terms, what the classics instruct us are the foes most difficult to best on the field of battle: that is to say, ambition and the plaudits of the general public. I would prefer a thousand times over to remain the excluded middle, as I heretofore have, to dwell in the shade of Plato's cave or that of the Porphyrian tree than to pace the public plazas of the world, slicing false Gordian knots—not, needless to say, with the sword (that symbol of power, with which I have nothing whatsoever to do) but even with the modest razor of Occam, however keen and subtle the latter may be. *Dixi*."

Naturally, this answer—recorded by an eyewitness with a pen so scrupulous that nary a comma has been added or omitted—as well as the protracted silence that stretched for several brief seconds in its wake, sends those crestfallen individuals off with tails tucked between their respective legs; as when, at end of day, through dying light, the flock, attentive to the shepherd's call, picks its hesitant path through the fields and returns to the fold.

E. TORRES: A SINGULAR CASE
by Luis Jerónimo Torres

CONTRARY to what the peculiar title of these reminiscences might seem to suggest, E. Torres is by no means a singular case in the land of his birth.

In his reverence for classical literature (always displayed with a sophisticated affectation), his sense of justice, and his wholesome virility (verging on garden-variety machismo, and celebrated by Tyrians and Trojans alike—their opinions thus reconciled for the first time in history), one sees scant difference between E. Torres and the majority of the editors of our newspapers' cultural supplements: men who offer the reader analyses of various foreign literary works and polemics, unsullied by the sorts of political themes that tend to corrupt, as Socrates had it, the youth, and which ultimately serve to do little more than divide the left from the right, so that, in the final analysis, neither side has any idea what the devil the other is up to.

Ever since founding the Sunday Cultural Supplement of *El Heraldo de San Blas*—a daily paper that, much like the light of those stars still observable by the telescopes of astronomers millions of years after extinction, continues to illuminate the hearths of the residents of San Blas even fifteen or twenty minutes after having been read—E. Torres has wholly transformed our journalism by gathering in said supplement's columns, without any distinction whatsoever of sex, morality, or ideology, not merely the fruits of our own state but the contributions of the younger generations of neighboring districts, not to mention the productions of various sons of San Blas living abroad, and Spaniards and Latin Americans domiciled here—since, after all, not everything has to be about resentment of the past, and there's no need to glut our collective attention with poorly understood quarrels and destabilizing scandals, forging a sort of artificial chaos where in fact a wholly natural and enjoyable chaos already exists.

As for myself, I have long since left San Blas behind and settled here, where I make my living as a journalist—I won't say ineffectually, but certainly with modesty. My ambitions as a novelist and poet have been abandoned, relegated to their proper place by economic necessity, overly affable friends, and a certain weakness—only too real!—for the cantina. I may not be in great demand as a journalist, but I know that I do have at least a handful of loyal readers. I enjoy a number of things about journalism—for instance, the great diversity of topics I'm able to address. One is always being presented with the opportunity to absorb oneself in some new subject: a book, a murder, a political act—and even from time to time the celebration of some individual who has achieved a higher rung on the ladder than oneself and with whom (as in the case now before us) one is more than intimate. Though it is impracticable here, of course, the possibility of writing under a pseudonym also appeals to me; and over the course of my career I have used a great number of them, perhaps dozens. On occasion even my closest friends have been oblivious to the fact that when we discuss a particular article the author they are mocking is none other than myself. Apart from providing amusement, such moments have taught me two things: first, humility; and second, that often enough the only thing that lends ideas their worth is the renown of the writer who presents them to the public. There's no point declaring that the world is fundamentally unjust if you haven't earned the right to launch such a platitude with the force of a newly discovered truth. Thus the reader should be advised that in the course of what follows, he will encounter pure and unadulterated truths that nonetheless grate on him, right from the get-go, since they are being imparted by someone utterly unfamiliar to him—not to mention the fact that everything there is to say about E. Torres has most likely been said already.

*

In order to substantiate these recollections, I embarked some three weeks ago on a return to San Blas, where I hadn't set foot for a number of years. Over the course of eight brief days I made an afternoon visit to city hall in search of a particular record (which I did not end up finding), rode the metro, attended a concert at the Bellas Artes, wandered through several museums, heard a talk by a prominent poet, watched a bullfight, paid a visit to a cheerful establishment much beloved in days gone by, where a pair of erstwhile lady friends gleefully reminisced with me about Eduardo and the mambo, and, finally, looked in on a few acquaintances of yore, all of whom agreed that I hadn't changed a bit.

San Blas!—that big city with all the charm of a small town, and vice versa. I thought of what it must have been like four hundred and fifty years ago, when Captain Pedro de Enciso was so wholly persuaded that the hill that now bears the name of San Blas (and which would later turn out to conceal a pyramid constructed in the pure Quipuhuaca style) held a rich vein of gold, in which belief he persisted for the remainder of his life. (Every schoolboy knows that before he expired, transfixed by the sword of his dear friend Luis de Olmedo, who was later hanged by Diego de Duero, who was slain by a ball from an arquebus during the desertion of Fernando de Oña, who was carried away in his turn by the gangrene consequent on a knife wound delivered by his brother-in-law, the famous Governor Velasco, on the occasion of the insurrection led by Anselmo de Toledo, which culminated in the massacre of nineteen traitors who met the same fate as their chief, García Diéguez de Paredes, a native of Huelva, Spain, and known to all and sundry as "Silver Hands" for his skill and expertise in the preparation of the finest Huelva chorizo to be found in the New World; I repeat, every schoolboy knows that before he expired, Pedro de Enciso laboriously raised himself from his deathbed, lifted his sword in one trembling hand, and, pointing it northward, pronounced the famous sentence that also constituted his final words, drawing the second of said words out for as long as he could, as though to prolong, be it only for a moment or two, the little life that remained to him: "The goooooooooooooold!"—a sentence for which, apart from a pair of finely worked funerary breastplates concealed within the pyramid, there was as it turned out absolutely no justification.)

Thus, thanks to the hallucination of a dying man, or with said delusion serving as a sort of cornerstone, San Blas was founded at the foot of this counterfeit hill, and baptized in honor of the saint on whose holy day it was established, in a capacious valley that was also christened San Blas—for it seems that neither Enciso's companions nor their successors were excessively burdened with imagination, so that the little stream that skirts the city became known as the San Blas River, and, indeed, today the local ballet is called the San Blas Ballet; the opera, the San Blas Opera; and the football stadium, the airport, the bullring, and the state itself are all named for San Blas; or perhaps the residents of the city chose that name, and continue to choose it today, because of all names, it is the most euphonious and easiest to remember: San Blas, S.B.

Now I have been asked to carry out this work, which I wouldn't dare to call an apologue or even a portrait, at a moment when age and exhaustion combine to prevent me from doing so not merely with the skill demanded by the subject but also with that proverbial modesty of the biographer which, I am sad to say, I entirely lack—for both the uneducated masses and the general public seem to believe that such an undertaking is a trifling thing, as though the example furnished by a Cervantes confronting the blank page of his prologue weren't more than enough to discourage a lesser biographer. Yet the road to success is well-paved with just such defective understandings.

What could I possibly say in praise of a sibling still among the living that wouldn't offend his modesty? And what could I say against him (since I have to admit that our ideas have often clashed, and that even now—in vino veritas, as usual—I'm certain that much of the fuss made over him is exaggerated) that wouldn't be seen as the fruit of fraternal envy for one who from youth onward overshadowed the rest of us?

To return to the topic at hand: There were five siblings in our family, almost all of them young ladies, apart from myself and my brother. But in the end this was wholly the work of Nature, rather than of Eduardo, so I won't dwell on the matter here.

Another thing: Only a genuine provincial is capable of appreciating the war being waged day and night in the provinces for one or the other of the two cultures. And the provinces *are* the nation, Eduardo would say. Only such a fatherland, he added, is capable of being faithful to itself—the thorniest of all fidelities. My brother, likewise, has always been faithful to his fidelity to himself: I am convinced he has never betrayed himself by entertaining the same idea or concept for more than an hour at a time, or for twenty-four hours at the most. I know that in scholarly and merely official discourse this is the aspect of his thought that is praised most highly for its originality. But he is unperturbed: Everyone knows exactly how much sincerity to ascribe to scholarly or official discourse, and if they didn't applaud him, he wouldn't be sure whether he'd said something true, false, or witty.

But to return to our subject.

My brother sprang ab ovo—or "from the egg," as Leda phrased it, according to Homer—in San Blas, the fruit of an easy birth. He was a strapping boy, though ugly, with legs much longer than normal, who slept soundly whenever he was afforded the opportunity. He cut his first tooth early on, but it is his first birthday that will forever be remembered—for at the precise moment the guests urged him to blow out the candle, an aunt let him fall (involuntarily, we suspect) to the floor, and it took nearly half an hour for him to regain consciousness. Later, our parents would fear that this fall had affected his mind, mainly because he reached the age of five without having uttered his first word—which was, in the end, neither "Papa" nor "Mama" but "book." From then on he spoke fluently, and learned to read in a month and a half. At first he would read whatever happened to fall into his hands, but especially those books and papers he came across in the street. Even today the employees of the public library remember marveling at the sight of that boy in short pants arriving each afternoon in search of volumes of history and science, several of which still bear the marks of his reading, particularly streaks of chocolate or, in certain cases, of a fainter substance that has been identified as an amalgam of caramel and saliva. There follow a number of years that remain obscure due to a lack of data or familial recollection, though we have evidence of the German measles as well as some mild and ultimately evanescent facial blemishes. The end of childhood coincided with an odd and unexpected lapse of sphincter control attributed by one family member at the time to the following causes: (a) lack of character; (b) caprice; (c) desire to annoy; (d) excess of character; (e) cold; (f) desire for attention; (g) paternal inheritance; (h) maternal inheritance; (i) lack of affection; (j) imitation of other children; (k) excessive coddling; (l) suffocating heat; (m) unknown causes; (n) excessive consumption of soft drinks, where applicable; (o) excessive consumption of spicy foods, where applicable; (p) night terrors; (q) insomnia; (r) a sense of neglect; (s) fatigue; (t) aggression; (u) concealed rage; (v) simple desire; (w) environmental allergies; (x) a recrudescence of the anal stage; (y) fantasy; (z) all of the above at once.

Here one is pleased to be able to note that from his very first day on earth Eduardo loved his parents deeply, wool carders though they were, and that very early on, despite the inclemency of the climate and a certain natural recalcitrance, he set about conditioning his spirit through a study of the classics—including the Greek, Spanish, and Latin authors. (In San Blas, his infantile translation of the apothegm "*dura lex, sed lex,*"

> Though the Law may run against you,
> Your duty is to obey—
> For both your immediate good
> And your honor are at stake.

which the Romans were quick to unlimber whenever they wanted to get their own way, is still fondly remembered.)

As for his youth, it is difficult to find anyone in San Blas who hasn't lost the opportunity to observe how extremely few were the books that his curiosity wouldn't deign to investigate, even in an environment where they were so scarce that, as E. Torres himself would say much later—on an unforgettable occasion that the state of my memory prevents me from recalling at this or, indeed, any other time—it was difficult, even impossible (to say it once and for all) not to encounter the nonexistence of the best and most rarefied works of our language, today (Friday) in decline, but in that era nearing its apogee. Thus we will allow ourselves to affirm that his classical education must have emerged more from his memory, as Plato didn't forget to note, than from his deficient environs; but it is likewise true that when one is possessed of such an insatiable thirst for knowledge, it is almost impossible to avoid the temptation—indeed, the natural yearning—to slake it.

And slake it Eduardo did, leaving himself with nothing more to investigate but the hereafter. Indeed, existence beyond the grave greatly fascinated him. Some of his most trenchant aphorisms—which, I am told, are only partly collected in this volume (there exist others; for instance, a rather revolting one relating to the attraction between the sexes)—constitute a hidden treasury of truths regarding life in the underworld.

Yet it must be acknowledged that the spiritual realm failed to detain him for long—since it is notoriously difficult for a restless spirit with its feet planted firmly on the earth to detach the former from the latter, in the absence of strong arguments. (An apology would be appropriate here, but given that digression is one of our little fortes, or temptations, we lack sufficient strength to abandon ourselves to the weakness of avoiding it.)

So it was that, having completed his classical education, E. Torres experienced, so to speak, his eureka moment and set out to wander the fields of the mind in an increasingly obstinate search for a decisive answer to the most urgent conundrums of our time, for which errand San Blas was not merely the best place in the world but also the most salubrious in terms of tranquillity of the spirit. And as the reader is certainly aware, matter may offer its produce to those who prefer it with good reason, but the spirit, too, unostentatiously supplies its portion, one that is not only sweeter but even more durable than those ancient trees, still bringing forth fruit, which, so prodigal of shade, surround on more than one side our suffering city.*

---

*Here concludes the manuscript of Luis Jerónimo Torres, who, driven by scruples of conscience, destroyed, in advance of his suicide, all material relating to the puberty and sexual life of E.T.

MEMORIES OF MY LIFE WITH A GREAT MAN

*by Luciano Zamora**

"We would be our own valets in order to be our own masters."

—J.-J. ROUSSEAU

1. READINGS

I'VE OFTEN remarked that a young man who devotes himself to reading is a young man lost—for whether he's caressing what lies beneath his navel, biting his fingernails until they bleed, or picking at his toes with his fingers, he'll spend days at a time stretched out on his bed, spinning who knows what sort of fantasies and sacrificing his time to his insatiable curiosity about (or enthusiasm or pity for) the human race; but the crowning sadness is that even if he's lucky enough to read Alexandre Dumas, he'll eventually forget about D'Artagnan; if he reads Victor Hugo, it is only a matter of time before he ceases to ponder the fate of the poor; and if he reads the story of Manon, it won't be long before the sufferings of unfortunate whores pass wholly from his mind.

To be clear—I, for my part, haven't forgotten any of these things. But I *have* come around to the belief that a young man who laughs in a policeman's face is probably mad; that generally speaking, the poor smell terrible; and that if you aren't careful, the whores will run off with the last pesos in your pocket. So it is that the feverish tears and excitements inspired by our youthful readings drift tranquilly away from us, like shadows, ships, and clouds.

*These memories are respectfully dedicated to Bárbara Jacobs.

From the day I arrived in San Blas from the countryside without so much as a peso to buy myself access to all those whims and diversions so coveted by youth, until the day when, years later, I abandoned the city in search of a brighter future, I served as secretary and *ayuda de cámara*, or valet—depending on what he preferred to label me at any particular moment—to Doctor Eduardo Torres, a man already too well-known, respected, and reviled in that miserable town for me to need to list his merits or eulogize his work, which is almost as widely diffused, praised, and vituperated as the man himself. Suffice it to say that even though the opinion currently held of him by the general public makes it impossible to say with any certainty whether at bottom the doctor was a vulgarian, a humorist, a sage, or a fool, the odds are that when he happened to come off as one of the four things mentioned above, some shade of the other three was never wholly lacking either. But I must declare once and for all that (valet or not), the doctor was a hero to me, as much for his almost encyclopedic knowledge as for his generosity and the sterling treatment that I always enjoyed at his hands.

It's common knowledge that during my years in his service the doctor insisted that I educate myself, so as eventually to make something of my life. But the truth is that despite his urging, I could never endure his various volumes of law or grammar for more than fifteen minutes at a stretch because what I liked best was to let my soul soar away on the wings of fantasy, and whenever he left the house in the morning, locking me up in the library, instead of perusing those seemingly inoffensive books I would snatch up the best novels of Jules Verne, Victor Hugo, Salgari, or—in another, more intimate genre—*La Dame aux Camélias*, devouring them from cover to cover; and not content with this, I'd tuck them into my pants or beneath my sweater whenever I could and sneak them back to my room at night without him or anyone else noticing, and often enough, dawn would surprise me poring over them by the wavering light of a candle which, by that hour, was generally on the point of guttering out.

I was seventeen years old. I can't say what force urged me on, but if I didn't spend the night reading I'd find myself beset by nightmares, or else I wouldn't be able to keep my eyes shut—and if I did happen to fall asleep for a bit, I'd wake the next morning so exhausted that I was incapable of doing my job properly, of helping the doctor don his coat or of fetching him his cane, and he'd realize that something was off and say to me, What's the matter, you little bastard, you've been masturbating again, haven't you, you're going to drive yourself crazy if you keep that up; and I, instead of saying yes (since in fact he was right!), would simply claim that I'd been studying civics, or our national emblems, or the borders of San Blas, and he'd act as if he believed me, and when he left he'd lock me up in the library again, since he always insisted that I was his *valet-secretary*, and not his servant.

He was a sweetheart, wasn't he? But I didn't realize it at the time.

2. VAGUE HINTS OF SOMETHING FAMILIAR

At moments like that, when one is so wholly absorbed in the world of books that everything else seems meaningless, or so irrelevant that it's barely worth mentioning, the Queen of Emotions is never far away: She may show her face in the afternoon, or at night, or as you're rounding the corner at daybreak—sooner or later, you can be sure she'll put in an appearance. I am alluding, of course, to Love.

Love, which had long pursued me like a shadow through novels and books of grammar (where it tended to crop up in specimen verses used to illustrate prosody), now began to announce its imminent appearance in the world beyond the page. If I happened to see a flower, for instance, I would find myself lost in reverie for who knows how long until some sudden noise brought me back to reality; if it was raining, so much the worse, for then I couldn't think of anything at all without being plunged into melancholy, who knows why, at the sight of raindrops running down the windowpane; and on a sunny afternoon, the mere flight of a fly (and how much more intensely if there were two of them playing together in the air!) brought on a strange sort of disquiet, so that my mind wheeled off on odd flights of its own, generally among vaguely feminine forms, forms whose indistinct faces seemed to smile at me from afar, whose arms stretched themselves suggestively in my direction, urging me closer, closer, so that I might be embraced.

What times!

3. FELICIA

To return to my theme: Back then, on that same Calle de Mercaderes where the doctor had his house, the lawyer Luis Alcocer lived with his peculiar family, comprised of his wife and his two daughters—only teenagers, the latter two, but already quite restless.

I'll say en passant that one day this family was joined by a live-in maid named, as I later learned, Felicia, a girl of around sixteen years old, of slightly less than medium height, with regular features remarkable for the absolute lack of suffering perceptible in them, abundant black hair which fell around her sensual shoulders in two thick plaits adorned with colored ribbons that lent a distinguished charm to the ensemble, full lips perpetually parted, moist, and drawn up into an enigmatic smile, half timid, half ironic—as if, behind the back of their owner, there loomed a wooded and rocky landscape—and black, languid eyes that seemed stirred by some great inner disquiet. Though she certainly wasn't tall, her body, thanks to its natural turgidity, was extremely attractive, and said attractiveness only increased when she walked through the streets on her errands, fetching bread or milk, swinging her hips to a strong, rapid rhythm, as if she were saying *Follow me*, or *Touch me*, or *Grab me*, but at the same time pretending not to know, pretending that it was all spontaneous, though I observed her, followed her nervously with my eyes, acting as if I didn't see, until she finally disappeared again into the house (though not before making sure that I'd been watching), laughing until she was fit to burst— all of which made me immediately and absolutely crazy about her.

4. HIDDEN MOTIVES

As regards our employers, I'm sorry to say that at this point in my life the endless backbiting and gossip circulating between the two families had fostered a great deal of ambient hatred, all of it egged on by neighbors, friends, and journalists, who were always the same in that sordid little town—that is to say, the journalists, friends, and neighbors were inevitably the same people—and sometimes it would be the neighbors, sometimes the journalists, sometimes the friends, who did the egging on, but they were always the same ones, and they all knew everything about everyone.

It was common knowledge in San Blas that Señora Torres and Señora Alcocer loathed each other; in spite of the fact that they saw each other daily, a tremendous hostility had grown between them, superficially owing to the professional rivalry of their respective spouses. But as always, it pays to dig a little deeper, so as to illuminate the hidden side of things (which are never quite what they seem, far from it, and a good thing too, for if they were there'd be no mystery at all, and life would be far too easy, far too bland), and I firmly believe that, deep down, each of these ladies preferred the other one's husband to her own, for although there's no question that the doctor enjoyed greater fame as a writer, the lawyer was also quite well-respected, and among the restless ladies of San Blas (all of them dying to tread the primrose path of dalliance, a handful dissuaded by dread of scandal), he was a renowned Lothario—several had abandoned their husbands for his sake, and various others, without going quite that far, had certainly slept with him—and the particulars of what he did to them were anybody's guess, but whatever it was, it drove them absolutely crazy; and what's more, he was a famous gambler (sometimes his game was poker, sometimes gin rummy, sometimes roulette), and it was said that on some nights he won thousands of pesos, whole mountains of cash, and that on others he'd lose everything, his house and land included, on a single throw, and his friends would sit there without a word while he locked himself in the men's room, as white as a sheet, and for several minutes they'd all remain motionless, waiting to hear the gunshot, but before long he'd emerge and serenely take his place at the table once more, and around dawn he'd win it all back with a hundred or two hundred pesos that someone had loaned him on his graduation ring, which was gold and engraved with the seal of the university.

But the contradictions of the human heart are many and varied: It was also whispered that Señora Alcocer, the wife of this great dandy, was simply dying to sleep with my employer, the doctor, precisely because he was a man wholly lacking in vices, peaceful, a homebody, with a reputation as an incorruptibly faithful husband, or at least as one utterly henpecked by his wife, which in the eyes of the other woman made him doubly disturbing and attractive—for the female is by nature a corruptor, there's nothing she detests more in a man than his virtue, and she'll do anything in her power to undermine it; but she is equally by nature a savior, and when she happens to observe another woman dominating her husband, an instinct that she has carried with her unaware since childhood rouses itself and she can't help wanting to liberate him from said domination at any cost, so as to be able to dominate him herself; and then, leaving the nature of women to one side, there is the simple allure of famous men, Lotharios or not, faithful or not, and even a little of said fascination drives the ladies so wild they simply have no choice but to hurl themselves at a celebrity, even if it often turns out that such famous men are considerably less manly than they'd imagined; but still, they're satisfied, and don't even notice the difference, it's enough for them that they possess their famous man, and that the rest of the ladies are burning with envy. And so it goes.

5. CULTURAL DUTIES

You yourself will surely have encountered, or seen from afar, various eminent men. Well, when people observe the great from a distance, who knows what they think; maybe they imagine that in everyday life the famous come across just as they do when they're performing some public act, or when they're beavering away in their office under the nation's flag or the president's portrait. Wrong. Whenever you see an eminent man in public, remember that he too is a human being—which is by no means a mark in his favor (far from it!) precisely because it means that he suffers from various defects, fears, weaknesses, manias, and eccentricities.

So it was with the doctor, who tended to be quite unassuming at home. The morning I presented myself to him, at my uncle's recommendation, my skills amounted to little more than a proficiency at typing, along with a bit of stenography. But in those days this made me a kind of local prodigy, and he immediately appointed me not merely as his valet or assistant, as had been arranged, but also as his private secretary, which instead of exhilarating me filled me with dread, for up until then I had never so much as set foot in that kind of private library, with all of its hardbound books, its portrait of Virgil, its maps of the world.

Well, that morning I found him alone in the midst of all that clutter, practicing a bit of fencing in his shirtsleeves, like any other gentleman in his own home at such an hour.

"It's wonderful that you know so much," he said, whipping the point of his sword back and forth between my eyes, in imitation of the fatal thrust of the Duc de Nevers. "I have so many things in need of organizing, copying, collating, sorting, revising, and archiving."

All this while alternating rapid leaps backward with two or three agile steps forward.

He soon showed me to his desk, very large, almost empty of papers, and covered with a thick sheet of glass in which the ceiling, the windows, and one's face lay reflected.

"Have a seat there," he gestured with his weapon, directing me to an enormous swivel chair. "Do you see that hole in the seat back?" he asked with a smile. "It was made by the bullet when my father shot himself."

Looking at the hole, all I could think of was everything that the bullet would have had to traverse before and after accomplishing its task: a coat, a shirt, an undershirt, skin, a muscle, a rib, a heart, a lung, another rib, another muscle, skin, an undershirt, a shirt, a coat, and, finally, the back of the chair.

"Here are today's newspapers," he added. "Take this pencil and mark everything cultural for me."

And he left without another word.

Now, back when I first arrived in San Blas, pretty much everything struck me as dazzlingly cultural, so that I agonized over my task during the first few days, marking every single thing I read, deathly afraid of slipping up and omitting some important item. But in time I realized that in fact very little actually qualified as cultural, and that what did, could generally be found in the columns located between the birthdays, the crime stories, and the wedding announcements, and my pencil accomplished its task with ease.

This left me whole mornings with nothing to do, and it was then that I reacquainted myself with the delights of novel-reading.

6. AN ASSIGNMENT

One morning a few days later, the doctor went to a large cabinet that served him as a bookcase and took from it a box made of mahogany, or what I judged to be mahogany, for back then any beautiful wood seemed like mahogany to me, since it was the type most often mentioned in novels (along with ebony, which was used when describing Negroes), the runner-up being pine, which generally appeared in the form of a coffin whenever the wife of a laborer died of tuberculosis in an impoverished quarter of some city in France or Russia and said laborer was forced to take charge of his four children while his boss was off celebrating Christmas, drinking champagne, surrounded by his family, the local prefect, and some twelve to fourteen friends.

Then he drew from the box a good quantity of handwritten letters of various sizes and colors and spread them out on the desk.

"I want you to copy these on the typewriter," he said. "I'm going to burn the originals. You, who are a man of the world, will be able to imagine why."

He said no more. He left the room, and I heard him locking the doors behind him, leaving me to my fate as a man of the world.

7. IMAGININGS

When the doctor stepped out and I heard the door lock behind him, I ignored the box, because a novel was always more attractive to me. In truth, I don't remember whether it was a novel or something else that seized my interest at the time, but after a few minutes I started to get bored, and began instead to ponder those things which were so constantly on my mind at the time. Above all, as is only natural (and little by little forgetting about the world around me), women— their legs and their breasts and generally speaking every sort of thing connected with them, it didn't matter what part it might be so long as it was part of a woman, but if it happened to be any of those parts in the front or the rear, so much the better. I can't say why exactly I never thought about the other two sides that women have to their bodies, although I did spend a fair amount of time pondering the mouth and the immense delights that it's capable of affording, whether in the form of kisses, smiles, or simple bites, or indeed the words that I imagined them saying to me when I closed my eyes, for example, "I love you," which isn't heard terribly often in real life but is precisely the sort of thing you think of when you think about having to say something to somebody, or what you imagine somebody saying to you, when you happen to think about such things. Nor did I dwell on the ears, because ears had never afforded me much pleasure, not even when I pushed my pinkie finger inside one of them for a scratch, though I've since learned that they're not to be sneered at if someone is willing to slip a tongue into one, but at the time I wasn't thinking about ears, rather about those parts in the front and the rear, and in no way could I force my thoughts beyond, except of course when it was a question of the Ultimate, which I certainly shouldn't mention here but which I'm well aware that everybody thinks about, having discovered over the years that the older people get, the more they think about it, until it reaches the point that, from the moment they get up in the morning to the moment they go to bed at night, they think of practically nothing else.

Afterward, calmer, my thoughts turned back to the box.

8. LONELINESS

Months passed, and I continued to devote myself to reading. Ever since childhood I had read whatever book happened to fall into my hands, but of course there hadn't been that many of them; now, when I was able to take my time with them, and when I wasn't preoccupied by those more than ambiguous fantasies mentioned above, it was novels that delighted me more and more, maybe because I was forced to read them in secret, and pleasure always is heightened by the nervous tension you feel in the pit of your stomach when you know you might be taken by surprise, so absorbed are you in your flight of fancy or sinful act.

Well, that's precisely how I enjoyed those solitary and forbidden readings. Nevertheless, as man is the oddest and most changeable of beings, I understand now that, while I was taking such morbid delight in my solitary enjoyment of the taboo, I was also beginning to feel the pressing need to share that solitude with someone else—a fact that today, seen from a distance and utterly surrounded as I am by my family while writing these lines on the doctor, cannot help but strike me as a great paradox. But then tell me, is there anything having to do with the soul of man that isn't at bottom strange and paradoxical?

9. URGENT NEEDS

The truth is that one evening, morning, or night, I don't remember which, I came to the conclusion that what I needed most was someone with whom I could share my readings and, why not admit it, my deepest thoughts, someone like myself with whom I could speak freely, pointing out the beauty of this or that particular passage and asking whether he'd noticed this, that, or the other; that I had reached the season of life when one needs a friend, not merely (as fathers tend to assume) to play pool with, or to go bowling with, or (when you begin to feel the itch) to pick up who knows what sort of women, prostitutes generally, because you frankly can't take it anymore and have this desperate desire to figure things out and so put yourself through all sorts of frightful ordeals in order to learn once and for all how to *do* the damned thing and feel like a man; but rather (and this is something that fathers never even suspect) someone with whom you can talk about what's happening in the books you're both reading; and sometimes it happens that you and your friend will wind up talking in the street until two in the morning, and when it comes time to return home you'll stand in the doorway together for hours, talking and talking, and then, still restless thanks to all of the thoughts bubbling through your head, you'll propose accompanying your friend the one block back to his house, and that one block will turn into several, one after another, and you'll tally them up in your head without caring, until finally you arrive once again at your friend's house and the whole process seems as if it's about to start over, since neither one of you really wants to leave the other, and since, in the cool of the night, or the heat of night and the light of the moon, as the case may be, you've been talking with such terrific enthusiasm about D'Artagnan, or the great Porthos, who despite his immense strength could no longer withstand the weight of the enormous stone he was holding back so that his companions might save themselves, and did in fact save themselves, though he himself was irremediably flattened.

All this sort of companionship I lacked, because at the doctor's house I was forbidden from going farther than the corner, added to which I was already getting up there in years, nineteen by now, and didn't have a single friend.

10. UNSEEN EARTHQUAKE

One spring afternoon I spent a good long time up on the roof terrace of the doctor's house, absorbed in my thoughts, which could assail me at any time no matter where I happened to be, for the occasions were few in which I ceased thinking altogether, whether I was preoccupied with the future and everything I lacked in order to make a decent life for myself, or the past and all of the things I'd experienced up until that point, and how the present would be different if things had happened otherwise, etc.; and so thoughts came and went, now in this form and now in that, but the brain itself never stopped spinning.

On this occasion I was contemplating the clouds that stood golden against the sky as the afternoon drew to its conclusion. All of a sudden I began to perceive within me, perhaps in my belly, my chest, or my head—well, in every part of my body, more or less, including the hands—an ill-defined restlessness, a sense of unease the likes of which I'd never experienced before, and could therefore find no way of explaining to myself, which is the most upsetting thing about such situations, because, in the moment, the chief thing that occurs to you is that you may be about to cash in your chips.

At first, as was my habit, I made use of my intellect, and by methodically setting things in order and putting two and two together concluded that I must be suffering from a stomachache, since at that period I was constantly suffering stomachaches, due to my nerves; next I thought that maybe I hadn't slept so well (as generally happened when I spent time thinking about the past or the future); finally, with a calmer mind, I deduced that the most probable explanation was that there was going to be an earthquake, since over the previous four years I'd discovered that I had, and still have to this day, the faculty of detecting an earthquake two or three thousandths of a second ahead of its advent; but on this occasion more than four minutes passed without an earthquake transpiring, while that disquiet of mine continued to needle me, and I could find no rational way to explain it, even though, as I've said, I mobilized all of the resources of my reason to establish that (a) the stomach couldn't be involved, since that particular illness was chronic; (b) it couldn't be my insomnia, since I was *always* sleepless thanks as much to my thoughts as my reading; and (c) an earthquake could be ruled out both by observable facts and by any seismograph, since time had passed and none had presented itself.

Well, to make a long story short, do you know what was causing the whole thing? Love.

11. MEMORIES

It's difficult to say precisely where one's memories of childhood end, but certainly one knows more or less when they begin, and there are even those who can remember themselves as newborns in the bassinet.

My own first memory is from around the age of four. We were having a party at the house, with neighbors, relatives, friends. Of the party as such I recall nothing, though I do remember a number of friends from that era and later. Others have faded from my memory, and who knows where they are now, and what they hoped for (or have finally ceased to hope for) from life: whether those who wanted to be actors are soldiers today, whether those who scoffed at the law wound up as judges, or whether those who dreamed of circling the globe have become sedentary fatalists. It may well be that every once in a while one of them will remember me, and on passing me in the street will recognize me and feel a desire to walk up and say, It's me, So-and-so, but in the end they find themselves prevented by who knows what sort of fear. And often I think of still others, who couldn't walk up to me in the street if they wished to. One of them drowned in the river somewhere around the age of eleven; another, who made it to twenty, was killed by a bullet, and I can never forget him because his name was Aquiles—that is, Achilles; another, older than me, who was very rich and always went around with the prettiest girls because he had it all—English suits, a bicycle, roller skates—died much older, near thirty, and he was a wonderful fellow: Whenever he got bored with skating in the park he'd lend me his roller skates for a while, and if I fell down he wouldn't make fun of me in front of the girls but instead would pretend to be distracted by something and, almost as if we'd planned it together, would look in the other direction, so that they didn't notice the spill I'd taken. Years later he died from drinking too much, and when I found out about it I felt somewhat conflicted, because back then, kindness aside, he had also been dating the girl that I secretly loved, and when we stopped seeing each other around, she and I, because she'd started to go to a school for rich people, she could never have imagined, nor could she imagine today, that each afternoon

I would walk several miles, all the way to the obelisk, just to be able to catch a glimpse of her during the thirty seconds that she passed by, in her father's car, with her father, on her way home from school.

12. PARTIES AND BEATINGS

But what I'd wanted to talk about was my memory from the age of four. The party itself, as I said, I've forgotten. Parties fade from the memory because each new one effaces the one before, just as (oddly enough) the beatings delivered to one by life are themselves, so to speak, serially eclipsed. Whenever you're on the receiving end of a beating, you say to yourself, Well, fine, this particular beating will be the last, because now I'm going to die of sadness; but then along comes another that drives the previous one from your mind, and so it continues until you've accumulated so many beatings that it's as if you're standing at the summit of a whole mountain of beatings that have been delivered to you by life; but from that point on a sort of descent begins, and though the old beatings are still capable of causing you pain even if you make that descent cautiously, there is a part of you that enjoys remembering them, if only because they remind you that you're still alive, or in any case, that you aren't dead yet.

13. CURIOSITY AND TREMBLING

In truth the only thing my memory retains from the party in question is that at some point I found myself under a table, examining with great curiosity a number of little pink bits that I held open with my fingers, so as to see better, for it was the first time in my life that I'd been in such proximity to them. I recall my curiosity better than I do the bits themselves, along with a certain vague sense of danger, though I was so wholly absorbed with poking around with my fingers that I barely noticed anything else, busily peering deeper inside, so as to figure out what else there might be in there. I recall seeing two little legs as well, between which hung a small pair of white underpants that either I myself or their owner had pulled down, and I went on alternately poking and looking at those pink bits until one of my aunts came and hauled the two of us violently out from under the table and started screaming at me and beating me across the knuckles.

And from this distance I can't remember whether it was the little girl, my aunt, or I myself who was trembling; but it's highly probable that this is the source of my belief that whenever there's going to be an earthquake, my hands begin to tremble, and I can sense it two or three thousandths of a second beforehand.

And likewise, when I'm about to fall in love.

14. *INCIPIT VITA NOVA*

Now on the roof terrace, gripped by a sense of unease which nearly drove me in my desperation to raise my clenched fists to my throat— as when a drowning man imagines the whole of his existence passing before his eyes over the course of a single interminable moment and says farewell to life, lamenting all that he might have done but didn't, whether out of natural indolence or some other reason, or rejoicing at the memory of the good things he's going to be leaving behind, or of the things that he was in fact able to accomplish, for instance helping an old woman cross the street, or taking a Sunday walk in the park while whistling a pretty tune, or licking a decent ice-cream cone—that sense of unease in which I was drowning almost drove me to raise my clenched fists to my throat—fists that nevertheless (thanks to one of those acts of unwilled will so common in moments of danger) I kept nonchalantly in the pockets of my pants, clutching in the right a key chain and in the left an antique coin that served me as a sort of talisman—gripped by that sense of unease, I repeat, I remained there for some time.

All at once, as though drawn by a magnet of enormous power, my gaze wandered slowly and, as it were, without my noticing it to the roof terrace of the house opposite, where it discovered, leaning indolently against a balustrade and looking directly at me, the woman who from that moment on (if, of course, it wasn't some other moment that I neglected to notice, for I am frequently distracted, and the most important things can happen to me as I daydream without my even realizing it) would become the one and only woman in my life—that is to say, my dream made flesh: Felicia, Felicia Hernández, today Felicia Hernández de Zamora*; Felicia, that unforgettable figure for whom I would abandon everything, position, fortune, illusions. Yes indeed. That woman with the tawny arms was none other than Felicia, staring fixedly at me with astonishment, as if she couldn't believe what she was seeing either—as if this were all a dream from which she too, unfortunately, would soon have to awake, staring at me for an eternity with that sleepwalker's look, until finally, moved perhaps by the emotion stirred by this ineffable experience, she wafted to me from afar a sweet smile, followed by an unexpectedly booming laugh, before turning and stepping back into her room, leaving me behind in utter perplexity.

Soon afterward, possessed by pleasure or a tremendous pain (I couldn't tell which, so strange was my state), I too returned thoughtfully to my room. But I read no more that day, and fell into a deep sleep, even as a dead body falls.

15. THE UNQUIET MIND

I read no more, neither that day nor during those that followed.

My mind during those days was like one of those flies that you find at some moments sitting uneasily on the ceiling rubbing its hands, and at others flitting anxiously around by the window without making up its mind to go out, or fixed to the wall, immobile, as though dead, and apparently oblivious to the various ills of this world, or in any old place that flies habitually frequent, except when they're melancholy or lovestruck and at wit's end, since in such circumstances they don't

---

*A real name, behind which my authentic pen name lies concealed.

feel much inclination to go out in the street or even to pass their time on the wall, much less read anything or listen to music, because this or that sentence, or such and such a song, will remind them, who knows why, of the fly that they didn't see yesterday and can't see today, and now they have no idea whether this fly loves them, or is going to the movies or some party with mutual friends, happy, without a thought for them, and no matter what they read or listen to it simply reminds them of this absent fly that may, who knows, be lost to them forever, and that's why they can't remain quietly on the ceiling, or the window, or the wall, their thoughts are fixed on nothing but that beloved fly, who even now may be walking hand in hand with someone else while they, sunk in total abandonment, are incapable of maintaining their calm for a single second, neither on the floor nor the wall nor on the bed nor any other place or situation in life, life being filled with so very many flies.

16. LETTERS

Sooner or later, of course, I had to get started on the letters. Thus there came a day when I took up the first of them, unfolded it, and read such-and-such, twentieth of July such-and-such, and after that, in a rather elegant hand, "*My love*," colon.

Well, I thought, this will be from Doña Carmela. But it was not from Doña Carmela, because the signature clearly read "Lucy"*:

My love:

I passed you this afternoon and you didn't even see me. When two souls meet, it is dreadful if one fails to notice the other. Or is it that you're no longer interested in me? Patricia told me that she'd seen you yesterday with Erlinda, but I couldn't care less, because I know that you're mine. Or is it merely her body that attracts you? If the body were all, the All would be

*A pseudonym.

perfect—but then, who doesn't have a body with legs, arms, breasts that inspire sculptors, poets, artists, and musicians? Yes, art is sublime, but sometimes such works inspire in me a kind of tedium. And what do I inspire in you?

Your Lucy

From the moment I saw it this letter drove me to reflect on the depths concealed by its apparent frivolity. What do we have here? I asked myself. Passion, jealousy, love, and an unquestionable disdain for art? Does this woman, I thought, actually lack an understanding of art? Is she incapable of appreciating anything beyond a bit of embroidery, an apple pie (or compote), a floral arrangement, or a hairdo teased in preparation for a party? All this the letter *seemed* to reveal with utter artlessness, but something about it continued to disturb me.

By this point the reader will have divined that that something was the word "breasts."

Three times I was forced to transcribe it, for whenever I reached the word "breasts" in the course of my task I grew confused and put down "pests," or "jests," or "tests" instead, until I realized that something was happening to me around that word in particular and I ruminated on why precisely this word out of all of the rest should be the one to trip me up, and why the signatory, Lucy, spoke of legs, arms, and breasts rather than heads, elbows, and feet, and I realized that behind that exalted philosophical talk about the All was concealed an insinuation of something far more tangible—that is to say, graspable.

But the truth was that neither the "legs" nor the "arms" produced in me the same emotion as the word "breasts," although the latter was cleverly camouflaged by the proximity of "sculptors" and "musicians," and I concluded that, in the last analysis, the letter from this so-called Lucy had been written for the sole purpose of drawing the reader's attention to those particular bits of anatomy that not everyone, to put it plainly, possesses. They are possessed by women, and by no means by all of them, for there are some that are scarcely detectable, and others that are so enormous that the mere act of calling them "breasts" would seem ludicrous; others hoist them excessively high, without realizing that such things are to be found nowhere in nature; others allow them to hang so low that they could almost be confounded with the belly; others completely abjure the bra and believe they look very pretty (and still others completely abjure the bra and *do*, in fact, look very pretty); in short, this letter with its mention of breasts opened my eyes and provided me with the key to numerous other matters, and ever since I've imagined that the majority of women spend their days inspecting their own breasts, from the left side, the right side, lifting them up with both hands, weighing them, evaluating them, and then bending forward or leaving one button of their shirt undone, so that you can't avoid seeing them; in other words, they think of nothing else. And so, I meditated, how much time could they have left over to appreciate art?

Well. As I continued to transcribe the letters, I allowed myself to read a good number of them, because curiosity got the better of me, and you know what curiosity is like. And all the more since I was alone in that library filled with busts of marble, with porcelain figurines of fauns and naked ladies, and little porcelain boxes decorated with *scènes galantes* and intended to hold who knows what, since they were always empty.

17. GOD'S PARDON

I was quick to observe that all the letters were love letters—if it's possible to call notes so full of hate "love letters"—and I felt lucky to have such work; I read them over and over, and thereby discovered what the various women who came so calmly to visit the house (mothers, aunts, female professors, lawyers, businesswomen, doctors, what have you) were actually like, or what they *had* been like at a certain stage of life, and I realized that all around me there was a world whose existence I had never suspected before, a world in which the usual courteous gestures, polite smiles, good manners, respectful glances, or simple indifferences melted away, revealing another, truer world: One more fascinating, harder, more dangerous, crueler, sadder, less secure, yet sometimes, nevertheless, richer in pleasures; a world in which all of those ladies lived so intensely, whether in their imaginations or in reality; so that now whenever I saw one of them in person, I would think, Señora, I read your letter a while back, and I know what you like to touch and what you like to kiss and what you like to do in the evenings when your husband isn't home or when you go out to see the doctor, and that you once wrote:

> I let your hands slide up my thighs and let our mouths meet in a kiss that couldn't have been a sin because at that moment I was thinking only of God, and God was allowing it so that we might purify ourselves, and who was I, after all, to oppose His designs.* NATY†

And so on, monotonously. Some were longer, some were shorter, but almost all of them were the same. In some of them, things weren't as well camouflaged as they were in the case of the arms, legs, and breasts, because I understood that it wasn't the same thing to say "legs" as it was to say "thighs," or to imagine a leg rather than a thigh. And indeed, whenever I came to those parts that mentioned thighs and breasts I couldn't stand it any longer and had to make a quick trip to the bathroom, where I ultimately spent a good deal of time pondering the fact that God understands and forgives everything, and while I was there I thought about how fine it was that God will, in fact, understand and forgive everything, because back then I still had a number of issues with God.

18. HUMAN INGRATITUDE

But I must return to the subject of these lines, which have been entrusted to me for the purpose of remembering my old benefactor;

*Quoted from memory.
†A pseudonym.

and how fine it is to remember him now, while he's still alive, for I'm certain that once dead he will be forgotten, like all great men who spend their lives burning the midnight oil for the betterment of a Humanity by whom they are neither appreciated nor, it could be said, even needed, except for the purpose of the occasional public appearance.

19. OBSESSIONS

I repeat that neither on that day nor on any of those that followed was I capable of reading a thing. From the moment our eyes met, Felicia had ceased to be, for me, a being of flesh and blood, of sensuous curves and turgid breasts, like any other; she had been transformed as if by magic into an obsession, by which I mean one of those ideas that suddenly takes hold of the mind, and whether you're out in the street, or at the movies, or at work, there's nothing you can do to shake free of it—for example, when you're seized by an urge to step only on particular paving stones, or when you can't make it farther than a single block before having to return home to check that the front door is locked or that you've remembered to turn off the gas or the kitchen tap, or whatever the damn thing might be; or, let's say, the fixed idea that you failed to address someone the way that you should have addressed them; or when you're a kid, the thought that you're going to go to hell because you fondled some particular part of your anatomy; or, when you're older, the conviction that you didn't say something you should have said, or that just when you should have said it, you said the opposite; until finally you forget that particular fixed idea, only to fall prey immediately to another: all those niggling feelings of guilt or anxiety that gnaw at our poor souls or, rather, to which our poor souls cling so as to feel, despite everything, that they actually exist.

But Felicia was something more than this, and I couldn't forget her.

20. TABULA RASA; AND: THE THREE THINGS THAT RULE THE WORLD

The fact is that the idea of Felicia razed from my mind every other impression, leaving it no more or less than a tabula rasa, or blackboard on which no one had written, but into which the auditory, olfactory (imaginary), visual, gustatory (imaginary), and tactile (imaginary) sensations relating to her were etched, as it were, on top of one another, with that disorder typical of the senses, until out of this confusion there emerged with dazzling clarity the skin, eyes, smile, contours, and graceful movements of she who had come to represent for me the very sum of beauty that could exist in the world, and particularly in San Blas, the capital of our state.

Yet over the course of my life I have learned—and it's a melancholy lesson—that there are only three things that rule the world, governing our actions and those of others, and these three things are Love, Hate, and Indifference, at times in a pure state, at others intermixed to a greater or lesser degree, but in any case, never wholly absent, perpetually weaving an invisible veil with which to entrap us, no longer in the form of an illusion, as the poets have it, or had it, but of a nightmare that prevents us from sleeping, perchance from dreaming. There you have it.

21. DIFFICULTIES OF COMMUNICATION (I)

Thus, I now found myself obsessed with making Felicia aware of my love for her. Naturally she didn't call herself Felicia, but I've taken to calling her that here because (as in the case of a man who, in his finest handwriting, sets down that he is committing suicide because it is in his best interests) it suits my interests to do so as long as there continue to live and breathe in San Blas any of the characters that feature in this story—which, by the way, I beg them not to believe a single word of, whether it be written, implied, or simply insinuated.

The important thing is that from the moment I saw her I couldn't go on living without her knowing that I loved her, in spite of the various hatreds subsisting between what—taking a certain poetic license—we could call our families, unaware as they were of the fire that was currently consuming "us." I highlight the word "us" here because I can't see with what right, if not that bestowed by inexperience, I could have supposed back then that Felicia felt in regard to myself anything more than the usual sort of sympathy or attraction proper to our ages or common professional interests.

22. LOVE, CARNAL AND PLATONIC

As far as I was concerned at the time, everybody knew that there was, on the one hand, Carnal Love, and on the other, Platonic Love. But of course, it isn't that simple. I'm sure now that my own love was Platonico-Carnal, or Carnal and Platonic at once, because whenever my thoughts turned to Felicia I felt something stir in the flesh, and likewise as soon as I felt something stir in the flesh my thoughts turned to her, so that I was continually passing from one to the other without paying it much mind or giving a thought to what variety of love I was experiencing at a particular moment or in what sense it accorded with these two philosophies, the Carnal and the Platonic. But as I allowed myself to suggest above, I know now that there also exists lovelessness—or pure and simple *non-love*—which could perhaps develop into Aristotelian-Carnal love, that is, the opposite of the Carnal but without rising to the level of the Platonic—remaining, rather, right in the middle, so that everything will be clear once and for all.

23. DIFFICULTIES OF COMMUNICATION (II)

You might imagine that there were plenty of occasions on which I was tempted to pick up the telephone, and plenty of occasions that I gave in to that temptation, and indeed I did; but the line was always busy, or the señora or one of her daughters answered, or the cook, depending on the hour. Then (it will have happened to you, too) I was forced to alter my voice, to pretend that I was a child or a woman, and ask some strange question or other, until at last the person on the other end grew suspicious and from then on simply picked up the receiver and waited, and I would listen quietly for a while before hanging up, slowly, as if they could actually see me slinking off. I had to give up this strategy one day when the señora, after a long silence during which only faint sounds, as of bracelets clinking and heavy breathing, were audible, shouted, "If that's you, Carmela, I'm coming after you!"

For the señora believed that Doña Carmela was still trying to talk with her husband, the lawyer Alcocer.

24. DIFFICULTIES OF COMMUNICATION (III)

Between this and other similar adventures, life went on for several days, which seemed to me like weeks, and with every day that passed I fell more and more in love.

Since you're no different from most people, the first thing that you'll want to know is why I didn't simply write Felicia a letter. Well, as a matter of fact, I did address various letters to Felicia, but from the very first all of these missives were skillfully intercepted, given that Felicia couldn't read on her own, so that every time the mailman delivered one of them she ran straight to the señora and asked her to read it.

I have to say that in the course of our whole courtship, this was the moment when we were in the worst danger of being found out. Nevertheless, since love conquers all, that danger was overcome thanks to the fact that in all my correspondence I never mentioned love, but rather various other things, such as her eyes, her body, and so forth; above and beyond which, I continually changed my pseudonyms, both as a simple ruse by which to keep her feminine curiosity piqued and because it was just more fun that way.

EPILOGUE

A great deal of time has passed.

Today Doctor Torres is honored with books and dissertations devoted to his work, and all sorts of tributes, like those on offer in this very publication. One might well say: Mission accomplished.

The lawyer Alcocer died in the bosom of his affectionate family, and not before repenting to the church (to which he bequeathed his final smile) for his sins.

As for me and Felicia, after pondering, outlining, delineating, and executing (or not) a thousand stratagems, such as the construction of a tunnel beneath the street that would deliver me into her arms, and which came to nothing because the few tools at my disposal, a spoon and an ivory comb, were insufficient for breaking through the sewage system that separated us; or the dispatching of messenger chickens from one rooftop to the other, chickens that, whether from lack of experience or the low density of the air, kept getting tangled up in the electrical wires above the street; at last I threw caution to the wind and simply presented myself at the house; I asked for Felicia, she came out, I proposed that she run away with me, she accepted, and that very same evening, with two or three cardboard boxes and a little bag in which she kept her jewelry, we left that inferno behind. With her natural talent she soon learned to read. Our children are a lawyer, an accountant, a sales manager (IBM), and a high-class flight attendant, who from time to time brings us souvenirs from places as far-flung as the islands of Malaysia.

IT'S ALWAYS HARD TO TALK ABOUT
A HUSBAND (A RECORDING)
by Carmen de Torres

So you ask me out of the blue, just like that, to tell you about Eduardo. Well, it's always hard to talk about a husband, because we women either love our spouses or hate them, and it even happens that sometimes they come to leave us indifferent.

Of course everyone is aware that Eduardo and I have known each other since we were very young, almost children; but back then he never gave me a glance, and I could barely bring myself to look at him, shy little thing that I was. Nevertheless, despite everything we would run into each other at parties and ice-cream parlors around the neighborhood, and after the usual cruising in cars, making as much noise as possible so that everyone would notice us, we started to go steady, like people do in San Blas society, until we finally got married, which was the only way of legalizing relations that would certainly have been stormy if it hadn't been for his steady temperament and my own patience, which allowed me to endure his constant reading and pretensions as a ladies' man, though I can't say for sure whether the latter ever proceeded as far as actual lovemaking or not, and it goes without saying that I wouldn't want to speculate—certainly not in a book like this—about such, well, let's say intimate details from back in those days, details that would, I assure you, I swear, immediately make the rounds of all the jokers in San Blas, where every woman knows who was whose lover or girlfriend, or, as they say nowadays in order to soften the sound of it, who "went" with whom, that's the phrase they use most around here to refer to people's personal affairs.

But the kind of jokes and gossip that are par for the course when you're dating someone in a little place like this (since no matter what people say, San Blas is still a small town, even if it *has* gotten a bit bigger) passed quickly in our case because we, well, because Eduardo and I were going together, and maybe a lot of people knew it, or maybe just a few knew it, but in either case the few or many who knew it had also been like us, in their time.

The real difficulties came later, once we set up house, when he started in with his work as a scholar in earnest, and didn't leave the house in the evenings at all and, as you can imagine, the children started arriving one after another, as if they had nothing better to do.

Eduardo was a real homebody back then and did plenty of reading, but in the evening there was nothing he liked better than a good snooze. I swear it's no exaggeration to say that he read so much in bed that sometimes he'd fall asleep with the book still in his hand, and the next morning when I woke up and stretched I'd feel something strange and hard there between the two of us, and it was usually a volume of some novel, even Cervantes.

You can see how hard it was, right from the beginning. Of course, I was well aware of a woman's proper role and did my best to keep house and adapt myself to his style of life, especially since sometimes, you know, it wasn't a serious kind of book like I mentioned before that he'd be poring over, but some lighter magazine, which is why, little by little, and because I felt the desire to be less stupid, I started to help with his work, and improve myself. Because this is exactly what so many people forget, and in fact it doesn't even occur to most women: the sort of responsibility that a wife is signing up for when she marries a man as famous as Eduardo, and one she's known her whole life. Afterward things get so complicated and so many problems crop up, and she annotates down* so many observations that almost without intending it she grows convinced that her husband is a great man, and once that happens she respects him to the bitter end and clings to him no matter what; or else it's driven home to her day after day that in fact such great men don't actually exist, that in fact he

---

*Presumably Señora Torres actually said "notes down," but the transcript of the recording fails to note this down.

simply has half the world fooled, and whenever people come to visit she hears him use the same sentence, or tell the same story, or the same joke, or the same anecdote with the exact same little words and gestures, until at last she knows them all by heart, and still she has no choice but to laugh, or to make some little comment as if it's the first time she's hearing it, in order to help him out, or at the very least to exclaim as if in admiration, "Oh, you!" so that the others think that she's simply bowled over by his ingenuity; or else he claims quite soberly that he's hard at work writing something of the utmost importance when in fact she knows that he's spent the whole week napping under the pretext that all the work he's been doing lately has worn him out, which she naturally doubts; and then, of course, she's always looking on, enraged, while he reads for hours and hours, day and night, continually scratching down notes, as if that were the only thing he had to do. You can imagine how utterly confusing all of this gets, until at last she has no idea what she really thinks about him. In my case, for example—Eduardo is so unassuming at home, I'm amazed at how often famous people show up from the most far-flung parts of the state, and even farther, in order to see him, and how, with two or three questions, only two or three damning little questions, you understand, about a book that's just been published or something like that, he puts them on the defensive from the moment they set foot in the door, even before they've had time to sit down. During the early years I didn't hesitate to stick my nose in, I'd tell him in front of everybody to cut it out, that he hadn't actually read such and such novel, but Eduardo would just roar with laughter, as if to let his visitors know that I was a real card; that's one of the ways he's found of solving the problem of living with a critical woman like me; still, he doesn't fool me; and yet I always have my doubts, and sometimes I wonder if, at the end of the day, it really *is* me who's the fool; believe me, it's difficult.

I remember that during the first few months of our marriage, Eduardo got a bee in his bonnet* about my reading more serious

*An expression that is still quite common in San Blas.

books of philosophy or literature so that I might be able to stay in the room and participate when he was receiving visitors, but the truth is that for folks from the provinces the style of *Siddhartha* or whatever can be rather difficult, so what I ended up doing was learning a handful of anecdotes about philosophers, like the one who was so regular in leaving his house at the same time every day that people could set their watches by him when he passed, or about some Polish musician or something, somebody famous in any case, whose lap I was supposed to have sat on once, so that all of Eduardo's intellectual friends would get the chance to make their witty double entendres or ask me whether it was just last week that I'd been sitting on his lap, and if I could tell them what it had been like. Anyway, if you keep company with that kind of person, something rubs off on you, even if it's just dirty little tricks, don't you think? [Laughter.]

But seriously, Eduardo receives every conceivable sort of book and magazine in the mail and I help him open them and put them away, and as long as you're paying the smallest bit of attention—well, a little more attention than that when it comes to paintings—*something* will stick with you, even if you're an idiot, and that's why from time to time you'll hear me mention some impressive name or other, even though if you were to dig a bit deeper you'd realize that I know about as much as Eduardo does himself. [Laughter.] You see why he says I'm a joker? Truly, I haven't been able to stop since back in my student days, when we cracked jokes constantly, even if I know that sometimes I only joke because I'm nervous, like now with this tape recorder of yours. But you promised that if I let slip any nonsense you'd cut it out, right?

Anyway, over time Eduardo began to write his articles for the newspaper and various other things, and he became a big deal in San Blas, but that must be because nobody around here knows anything, and frankly I couldn't care less if they find out that I said so because they all say it too, and it's better to say it about them before they have the chance to say it about you. To my mind they're a bunch of phonies, my husband as much as any of them, jawing on and on and on about his lofty subjects (oh me!) but hardly ever helping out with the chil-

dren, leaving them to me, or when he did, it was only to tell them to
read such and such book, as if that would do them any good at all,
or fill their stomachs, even though nothing was ever lacking in our
household in that respect, and thank God they're all grown up now
and none of them turned out like him. I've never minced words, I've
always said to him: What do you and your pals do, exactly? You spend
all your time at the bar or café talking the same nonsense and amusing yourself with people who imagine they're writers or God knows
what, while the rest of us are back home dealing with the servants,
and we certainly aren't getting paid for it. And don't even get me
started on the subject of servants, which I'm sorry to say is the only
subject that women in San Blas have any idea how to talk about.

Anyway, as I was saying, every time Eduardo wrote something he
got more and more famous, and meanwhile he was getting his law
degree at the university, but once he graduated (he was almost thirty
years old, the slacker) he never had the slightest interest in practicing
his profession because he was busy day and night with literature and
philosophy and political issues here and abroad, and whatever else.
Still, I can't complain, because the truth is that it's safer this way, he
can just stay at home instead of knocking around the streets chasing
ambulances or, as he puts it, throwing poor helpless widows out of
their homes on behalf of others, and besides, I know that he didn't
study the law because he *liked* it but because poets and writers around
here always become lawyers so that they'll be able to work in the
diplomatic service or some piddling ministry, or maybe he just did it
to please his dad, who was always pushing him to get a professional
degree, he never stopped repeating it, and I believe he was right about
that, because just as people will look at the clothes you're wearing
and treat you accordingly, a degree will open a lot of doors, even if
Eduardo is always claiming that the only doors he's interested in are
the Doors of Light, which, according to him, are open books.

Later, when the boys were older and we'd moved into this house,
which his father left him when he died, I found myself faced with
another of those ordeals that plague a woman who is married to an
intellectual—I mean the books, which Eduardo simply adores, though

I have to admit I've had it up to here with the task of opening the ones that arrive with uncut pages, and also with the dust that the maid is constantly sweeping off of them. The house immediately began to fill with hardback and paperback volumes of every sort that Eduardo found in the secondhand bookstores he'd frequent each afternoon without fail in those days on whatever pretext or in the company of whatever friend. Home he'd come, laden with supposedly rare editions, mostly of obscure poets from other provinces or states, and sometimes even from San Blas itself, which he claimed that he'd bought (remember, I'm talking about a long time ago) for twenty centavos or a toston, whatever would work as an excuse or a lie, so that I wouldn't get upset about the expense; he'd try to convince me that he'd stumbled across a bargain, that the books were really worth much more, and that they'd only gain in value over time, just like the paintings, though the latter were usually gifts from his painter friends, and he had to hang them up even if he didn't like them, well, I mean the ones by the painters who were still alive, or who lived nearby, since they sometimes dropped in unannounced, and if they didn't see them hanging in the parlor they'd think he'd sold them, and ask, What have you done with my painting?; although when people come over and see all those long rows of books on the shelves, he assures them, the ones who know about books anyway, that he bought them for a ridiculously low sum of money, so that they'll be jealous, I think, and marvel at how lucky he is when he goes to the bookstores; and he tells others, the ones he considers stupider, that the books cost a small fortune, but of course they already know that buying books is the worst sort of investment because nobody ever wants to give you anything for them when you're ready to sell, and then he says that as soon as he dies it's certain that I (and here he shoots me a malicious look) will go and flog them to some rare bookseller for whatever I can get, like the widows of all great writers do, and when they hear that, they always give me a courteous smile in order to show they're in on the joke, and they say that No, they're sure I know what those books are worth; but if you want the truth, I'm really not sure *what* I'll do when the time comes, because they say that the government isn't interested in buying writers' libraries any longer no matter how valuable they are—well, anyway, they claim that there are just too many of them out there and that they all contain the same books with the same dedications, and they aren't interested in duplicates, though Eduardo for his part insists that just as you can't find two identical fingerprints among common criminals, it's still indeed possible for the government to discover a good library, since no two libraries are exactly alike, and what a coincidence that whenever he goes to a friend's house they catch him examining the books and comparing them to his own collection and tallying up all the ones that he's missing, and his friends do the same when they come over here; and in his determination not to let the books push him out of his own home he's thrown away whole heaps of duplicates, because most of the publishing houses send him packages of new books and sometimes the authors will send the same ones with dedications, and because he's of the opinion that there's no such thing as a bad book (of course sometimes he contradicts himself and says that he'd like to give away all of them that don't have anything to do with his area of expertise, and after he's extracted them from the shelves and piled them up to go he repents and after eight days or so puts them all back where they were before, and then he's calm again, and sometimes I catch him gently caressing their spines as though he's apologizing to them, as if he regrets what he was about to do from the bottom of his heart, and I pretend that I was only adjusting a vase and didn't notice a thing, and I leave again without saying a word, because everyone has their little eccentricities, don't they? I get the same way about my clothes or the things in the kitchen, even if I don't wear them or use them any longer I don't get rid of them or give them to someone who needs them more than I do, because I'm thinking that I might want them again someday even if I can't stand them at the moment, you know how people are), he keeps them all, except for the duplicates, as I said, which he donates in small batches to the university or some other educational institution where students or poor people can come and see them. What he really loves are *libros empastados*, hardbound books, and it drives me absolutely crazy, and I tell him that he ought to steer clear of the *pasta*, it'll make him fat [laughter]; all joking aside, he already has at least six thousand two hundred of them bound in leather or something like that. His preferred colors are blue and red, and in fact they look quite nice packed together on the shelves and attract the attention of everyone who visits the house; I don't exactly love them myself, but even I have to admit that they're easy on the eyes; Eduardo sometimes admits that it's vulgar, the way he uses books as ornaments, that in fact for him books *are* ornaments, but of course in this as in so many other things, though it may be true, nobody believes him, they just laugh. The uniform collected works are also very pretty (though they already barely fit, and who knows if in the end and despite everything they'll wind up pushing us out of the house and forcing us to rent an apartment, hopefully one next door, so that he can be close to his library when death comes, I don't even want to think about all that, as long as we get the trusteeship set up in time I can monitor the whole thing from there without being intrusive, so that they don't drag everything away, but I don't want to get ahead of myself), and he explains that he buys them, as well as the complete works of all his authors in several languages, because he writes so much and at any moment he might need to consult them to resolve a question, or find some citation or whatever. For my part I think that this worship of books has become a mania for Eduardo, I mean just look at the volume of magazines he buys and the newspaper supplements that he skims quickly or peruses at length, depending, and that he hoards with that obsession he has for anything printed, no matter what it may be. But Eduardo isn't a practical man, he lives in his ideas; for him it's culture that matters, and that's all, which is why, incidentally, we live in poverty, as you see: genteel poverty, but poverty all the same. Just think of the kinds of official positions that have been held by people with libraries even smaller than his! But he's content with his Cincinnatus and his free-and-easy life, as if that were something you could eat. Sometimes I get fed up with it and tell him to look at so-and-so, they have it pretty good, don't they, without having to live like this, but later I feel bad about it, this is the cross I chose to bear, and there's really nothing to be done about it, right?

Our social life? What should I say. Generally we get a lot of people here, very formal visits that Eduardo receives as part of his work, or should I say his ministry (yeah, right). But social life in the strict sense? Almost none, really. Every now and then we get together here or elsewhere with a few of Eduardo's colleagues. Sometimes they come to the house with their ladies around noon, and I really prefer that, because then they leave before it gets too late, you get the chance to tidy up a bit, and Eduardo can turn in when he feels like it, and the next day he's in fine fettle, ready for reading or taking his walk; we're usually talking about groups of eight or so people who might already be friendly with one another, or not, as the case may be. If they're friends things are easier, you can predict when they'll get serious or silent, but we always try to prevent that from happening in the first place by playing some loud music by one of the great maestros, or some lighter American stuff—well, it makes things less difficult even if the guests are still a bit boring, especially when they're the kind of friends who see each other constantly and know all of each other's peculiarities and jokes and how they'll respond to everything, and nevertheless they still laugh, and I have to laugh too, so that they'll know I'm not stupid and that the jokes aren't going over my head. Sometimes the evening get-togethers are mixed, I mean, there'll be friends and then one or two new couples who live in San Blas, or are just passing through. There are plenty of the latter because Eduardo's friends abroad are always giving people his phone number so that as soon as they arrive they can call him up and he can help them solve whatever problem it is they're having, or else (because he's so nice, you see) so that they can simply drop in, because everyone knows he'll just be thrilled to meet new people, as if he has endless leisure to squire them around to the local pyramid or temple, or to the ballet. That kind of get-together, which might seem more difficult, isn't actually so bad, because right away you simply introduce the locals to the people passing through, and from there they take care of all the conversation themselves, which generally revolves around what such and such word means in such and such country, and which words are bad words in such and such place, and the rather amusing predicaments that it gives rise to, particularly if the person in question is an ambassador or is giving a lecture or something without having been informed of such land mines beforehand, and winds up saying something so vulgar or insolent or obscene right in the middle of the ministry or embassy that everyone just stares, or some barbarity that makes the president's wife blush and hurry to raise her neckline or lower her hemline, or whatever; or else they talk about common friends who you weren't aware are living nowadays in some other country, or who you weren't aware are now divorced, though honestly you probably could've seen it coming, since he drank so much, or she drank so much, or what have you; and other good topics are pollution, or the oil crisis, and how the widespread adoption of bicycles will ameliorate both problems, but eventually Eduardo gets bored with all that and says that the proper campaign isn't against noise or smoke but against human stupidity, and the others laugh, giving Eduardo the opportunity to tell some anecdote that, as I explain to him, I already know by heart, or else he tries to bring everyone into agreement with that air of self-seriousness that makes me burst out laughing whenever I see it.

Well, I've been talking about the kind of dinners that here in San Blas we call *sentados*, or formal, with candles to make everything look prettier and the two maids in starched uniforms serving from the left side and collecting the plates from the right side, which causes plenty of annoying problems given their ignorance of which side is which, and I have to stand there shooting them furious looks to remind them. But sometimes we also get together in the evenings more informally, maybe twenty or twenty-five people plus the waiter, who you don't hire in order to show off, like some people think, but rather to help serve the drinks and empty the ashtrays, at least at first, because later on everybody's more at ease and they serve themselves and do whatever they want with their cigarettes; but really we don't throw many of those kind of parties because Eduardo gets carried away with the booze and then sleeps a lot, and since he's usually an early riser he spends the whole next day complaining, but I don't say anything to him about all that because it only makes matters worse. Generally speaking the part of our social life we like best are the cultural events, the exhibition openings (whether they're modern or ancient), concerts and opening nights at the opera (the national opera, too), and honestly it's a real shame that we almost never actually get to go because of the distance and the problems with traffic and parking that make it easier to go all the way to another city than to get downtown, and the same goes for the movies and above all the theater, which Eduardo loves more than anything, but which we almost always have to do without for the exact same reasons if ever anything good is playing, but in fact there are almost never any decent cultural events around here. Another thing: The educated public isn't terribly abundant, so you have to divide or multiply when there are various cultural events happening at the same time; for instance, if on a certain day there are events in two different locations, they have to vary their starting times by at least half an hour, because if people aren't sure where to go and so choose the philosopher giving a lecture, they'll offend the poet who's giving a reading, and if there are three (let's say a painter having a show somewhere else), so much the worse, because then the first two lose out, and in a case like that people have to get in their cars and race as fast as they can from one event to the next in order to show themselves for at least a minute or two and so stay in good odor with all three, or else arouse the sort of jealousy that is (let's face it) inevitable in the course of any career.

Well, a typical day in the life of Lalo is more or less like any other day. He gets up very early, when the first roosters start crowing. His brother—who, so I hear, also wrote something or other for you—used to say that, like Archimedes, Eduardo likes to write in the bath, and that when some great idea occurs to him he leaps right out and goes running into the street, shouting I don't know what, or maybe it's more like Marat when he received his well-deserved comeuppance from Charlotte in Weimar, only halfway out of the tub; but if you want to know the truth, and you promise not to spread it around, I've never seen him do anything like that myself. No, when he finishes bathing he always leaves the tub and has his breakfast, and waits for the newspapers to arrive, and when they come he reads them thoroughly except for the sections on crime, which he has no taste for, and sports, which he prefers to watch on television whenever he has a few moments of leisure, which is pretty much always; what he reads with the deepest interest are the so-called *editorials*, in order to confirm his judgments, but he never agrees with any of them because of how intransigent he is when it comes to other people's opinions, even though he's always saying that he would give his life to ensure that others have the right to give their lives for their ideas; next he steps into the library and spends a while gazing at his books from a distance, and if thanks to some carelessness or neglect this or that volume isn't where it's supposed to be—and even if it is, as he sometimes jokes— he takes a moment to put it right again; then he chooses one of them and settles himself in his favorite chair where he reads from eleven o'clock in the morning until it starts to get hot; at which point he picks up his hat and walking stick and leaves for his morning walk in the park where he observes nature for a while (oh sure) or else strolls around for a while, reading very seriously, or runs into various other crackpots like himself with whom he discusses the day's news or some passage from the book he's carrying or whatever it is that one of his friends has just published. Around one o'clock he returns home exhausted, poor thing, and the maid knows that as soon as he gets in it's her job to bring him his soda. After he rests a bit, always while reading, he and I eat together, just the two of us, except when one of the boys happens to stop by, usually with his wife and kids in tow, and then we have to put a bunch of extra plates out, and it turns into a big production if you'll pardon my saying so. After we eat there's the siesta, which he never misses, given that he's always so tired—poor Eduardo, the truth is I think he's been looking especially knackered

lately, maybe it's the heat. Around five, by that point somewhat re-
stored, he returns to the library to read or to write down some of the
stuff that's always occurring to him (that's another thing: sometimes
in the middle of the night he'll wake up, turn on the light for a few
moments, write something down on a little scrap of paper, then go
back to sleep, and now and then he'll wake up again to repeat the
operation, and what kind of pleasure I get from this I'm sure you can
imagine; but he always explains to me that he has to do it that way
because if he doesn't write it down immediately he'll never remember
it the next morning), and in the end I have no idea whether he's writing in earnest or in jest because when people read what he's put down
they always end up laughing. When nothing in particular occurs to
him, he simply writes down his thoughts. If everything goes well, the
evening passes peacefully while everyone else in the house tiptoes
around him and he goes on reading and writing, ignoring the telephone, and when it rings I'm always careful to say that he's not there
or to take messages for him. But a lot of the time somebody ends up
stopping by without warning, generally young writers from San Blas,
female and male, who bring him their works either so that he can tell
them how they are or so that they can ask him for a foreword or an
introduction to a publisher or a letter of recommendation for a schol-
arship. I honestly believe that even though he moans and groans he
really likes it, because he always receives them very kindly and invites
them to stay awhile and asks them all sorts of questions—what books
they like best, whether they've read such and such, and things like
that; I know because I used to hang around and offer them coffee,
but after a while I got bored because the questions were always the
same, and so were the answers. Whenever they happen to be inexpe-
rienced young men he's very attentive and listens to whatever they
have to say, and finally, after consulting his calendar, he asks them to
leave their manuscripts and come back after about fifteen days; and
with the women he's even more chivalrous and spends a good long
time with them, being extremely solicitous, the old lech, never once
taking his eyes off the legs of those floozies who could certainly think
of something more useful to do with their time and leave such stuff

to the men, but in the end, he begs them too to return in a few days, or weeks, depending on the number of pages. I really don't know whether in Eduardo's case it's a question of hypocrisy or what, but the fact is that he's still never told anyone that their book is no good; on the contrary, generally speaking he always says very nice things, that they should continue down the path that they're on, etc., etc. There are plenty of anecdotes about all of this knocking around San Blas; for instance that sometimes, when they come back for their second visit, he declares the short-story writers to be excellent poets, and the poets to be excellent writers of stories; but they're so cowed by him thanks to his influence here in San Blas and especially abroad that they don't get offended, even though they must leave with the impression that he hasn't read a word of what they gave him; but who cares, they're wonderful people, aren't they, all of those loafers who come to steal his time, as if he still had his whole life ahead of him. When they finally go on their way and it's nighttime in earnest, he likes to sit alone and listen to a bit of music, local stuff, or else Beethoven, until fatigue sets in and he starts to nod off. Then, since I know him so well, and know exactly what's happening just as if I were seeing it with my own eyes, I call softly from the bedroom, "Lalo, Lalo, it's getting late," to which he responds that Yes, he's coming, and not long after, rubbing his eyes, which he can't keep open for exhaustion, and almost dragging his feet, and without even having a snack, because if you want to know the truth, food is the least interesting thing in the world to him, he comes into our room, where I've already made up the bed with fresh sheets, always with a book under his arm; then he undresses and lays himself down somewhat laboriously, and after reading for a few more minutes, and sometimes without even saying, Good night, Carmela, he falls fast asleep with the book on his chest, imagining who knows what, the old rogue, because sometimes he laughs while he's dreaming, wearing this expression that's very much like him, as if he wouldn't kill a fly, and which, if you want to know the truth, and no matter what else he may be, makes me love him more than ever and put up with all of his quirks.

PART II: SELECTIONS FROM THE WORK OF EDUARDO TORRES

A NEW EDITION OF THE *QUIXOTE*

THANKS to the special assistance (for which we express the utmost gratitude) of our distinguished collaborator, jurist, and man of letters, Don Damián González—always attentive to these matters of the spirit—we have lately received a beautiful copy of the novel *Don Quixote* by the renowned, indeed classic, peninsular author Don Miguel de Cervantes Saavedra, recently released by a prestigious Chilean publisher.

Though we're aware that critics in the capital have already commented on this volume, and though we recognize that pens greater than our own have dealt with it both on the Peninsula itself and in various other parts of the world—for it has been translated into languages as or even more sonorous than our own—we would certainly not want to miss the opportunity to proffer a brief commentary on this valuable work, which was the solace of our restless youth and remains an instructor in our years of maturity.

Few indeed are the novels that instruct us so delightfully, and fewer still those of which one may justly say that *castigat ridendo mores*, as old Juvenal put it. Nor has there ever been an author as misunderstood as the late Cripple of Lepanto, so cleped because of the hurt he received during the battle of the same name, and in which, as is well known, the Invincible Armada was vanquished not by the wretched and envious ships of the enemy but rather by the elements, scheming against the glory of the regiments of Flanders. But here, without wishing to, we have strayed from our theme.

Though it is true that Cervantes chose a madman for the protagonist of his work, it would be unjust to suppose that this generous spirit thereby intended to mock an unfortunate lunatic who had not harmed him in the slightest. No; behind this, there is more. Camouflaged by the apparent follies of the famous Knight of the Sad Countenance, as he called himself, exceptional spirits will discover various sublime passages dedicated to attacking novels of chivalry, a baneful literature which, as the author takes care to stress, goes hand in hand with the corruption of tradition and distracts housewives from the domestic duties in which they would otherwise be absorbed.

But even this would be a negligible achievement if the Divine Cripple, overleaping his own ideals, had not had the skill to create with his masterful pen the picturesque figure of Sancho Panza, a coarse and contemptible peasant wholly dedicated to the satisfaction of his basest physical desires, such as eating and sleeping, in contrast with the elevated virtues of his master, the originator of platonic love and a man for whom combat was rest.

Special mention should be made of the book's most famous adventures, such as those of the windmills, the rams, and the fulling-mill hammers, where laughter goes hand in hand with tears, and philosophical reflection with a profound understanding of the fickleness of the human heart. What other aspects of Cervantes's intentions in his immortal work have yet to be fully plumbed? We leave it to the scholars. For now, we will merely attend to this new edition.

But before we draw to a close, allow us to make a point no less conclusive for being penultimate: It is to be hoped that this magnificent work will be read by our youth, that youth which nowadays thinks only of dancing, when not about sports! We must also lament several obvious misprints in this edition that do tremendous harm to the prestige of so great an author. For instance, on page 38, we find the protagonist saying "*fuyan*" rather than "*huyan*" (flee) as is correct; further on, a "*hideputa*" (son of a whore) offends the eye. What must have been meant was . . . but we don't want to injure the ears of our delicate young ladies.

And then, one final qualm—a qualm that might seem trifling but is only meant to point out the ill (in keeping with the motto of this journal) wherever that ill may be found: In one chapter Sancho Panza is robbed of his beloved donkey, yet some time afterward appears mounted on it again, without our having been told how such a thing could possibly have come about. We find wholly insufficient the explanation later supplied to us by the author, for if he himself noticed the error, why did he fail to amend it in later editions, by which action we all would have gained? Such flaws are, of course, mere beauty marks, *peccata minuta* let us say, which in no sense sully the unfading glory of the most lay genius to have graced our language, one of the best and most musical in the world.

Reprinted from Revista de la Universidad de México, *vol. XIII, no. 5, January 1959; originally published in the Literary Supplement of* El Heraldo de San Blas, *San Blas, S.B., November 8, 1958.*

CARTA CENSORIA ON THE FOREGOING ESSAY
by F.R.

Mr. Director
Jaime García Terrés

My dear sir:

I sincerely believe that given the high quality of your interesting magazine, extreme care ought to be taken when it comes to the selection of manuscripts to be published.

Accustomed as I am to reading in the pages of *Revista de la Universidad de México* material that is (generally speaking) excellent, I was taken aback by the article published on page ten of issue 5, vol. XIII, dated January of this year.

Said article was written by one Señor Eduardo Torres and reprinted from *El Heraldo de San Blas*. I do not doubt Señor Torres's love for Cervantes's oeuvre, but I certainly question the wisdom of reproducing an article so plagued with ridiculous errors in a journal as prestigious as your own.

Among the many mistakes we might point to, a number of "necessarily fatal" blunders stand out—blunders that I believe even a high schooler would be incapable of committing. When Señor Torres refers to Cervantes as the Cripple of Lepanto, he pitiably confuses the battle of the same name (1571, at Lepanto, off the southern coast of Greece—a tremendous defeat of the Turks by the combined fleets of Spain, Venice, and the pope, commanded as you're well aware by Don Juan de Austria) with the loss of the Invincible Armada near Plymouth, England, which put an end to Spanish maritime supremacy, and which occurred in 1588. Of course we all know that Cervantes never served in the Armada, and it should be clear to Señor Torres as well, even if only by logic, that at the age of forty-one, as Don Miguel was then, and wracked with the ailments brought on by his years of captivity and privation, not to mention the loss of an arm, that it is wholly improbable that he could have been on the front lines at Plymouth.

Señor Torres calls our attention to what he considers errata in Cervantes: the words "*fuir*" and "*hideputa*." Even today, the *Diccionario de la Lengua Española*, whose lack of flexibility is notorious, admits as archaisms such words as: *fuir* = *huir*, *fumo* = *humo*, *fijo* = *hijo*, *figo* = *higo* (flee; smoke; son; fig). We continue on a daily basis to use the word "*fugitivo*," with its root in the verb "*fugir*." With respect to "*hideputa*," one finds in the dictionary the following entry: "Hi.—abbreviation for *hijo*. Used only in the term *hidalgo* and its derivatives, and in such expressions as *hi de puta*, *hi de perro*."

For another thing, the above is not the only case of its kind. We still use words like "*hidalgo*" (*fijo de algo*, *fidalgo*) and, much more commonly, "*usted*" (*vuestra merced*, *vusarcé*, *vusted*).

To satisfy himself on the subject of what might seem to him whimsical derivations, I recommend that Señor Torres consult the *Historical Grammar* of Señor Miguel Asín y Palacios. If even today such turns of phrase are accepted as archaisms, they were presumably commonplace in the sixteenth century. So that I think Señor Torres may rest easy as regards the wounds that such words might inflict on his delicate vision.

In bringing his brilliant article to a close, Señor Torres says that Cervantes is "the most *lay* genius to have graced our language." It is unclear if by this Señor Torres means *lay* in the sense of lacking clerical orders—but if so, I find his use of the comparative "most" here inexplicable. In this sense one is either lay or one isn't. "Lay" in the sense of untrained or amateur seems to me somewhat unjust to poor Cervantes. "Lay" in the sense of the Greek "*laikós*"—popular— well, I don't know how popular he would have been in his time. It is difficult to be popular when your book has not been widely disseminated among the public. In his own time Cervantes was certainly renowned but (alas!) very little read.

As for describing Sancho as a "coarse and contemptible peasant wholly dedicated to the satisfaction of his basest physical desires, such as eating and sleeping"—poor Sancho! Coarse, yes, but by no means contemptible. Sancho the good, the guileless, the unswervingly loyal; sarcastic and snide, but affectionate and honest. Gluttonous when circumstances allow, but generally content with bread and an onion. Sancho, who walked away from his governorship as naked as the day he was born, asking merely for half a loaf of bread and half a wheel of cheese as his viaticum, who governed according to what he knew and resigned with dignity, was anything but contemptible. Poor Sancho! No one has ever treated you so callously.

In conclusion, I would like to point out that this letter is not the product of a critic's pen. On the contrary, as an assiduous and enthusiastic reader of your journal, I merely hope that my modest contribution may in the future prevent articles such as the one addressed here from slipping in among the generally accomplished works with which you provide us.

My sincere gratitude for your attention, and I am pleased to sign myself your att. and aff. h.s.,

F.R.

Reprinted from Revista de la Universidad de México, *vol. XIII, no. 8, April 1959.*

TRANSLATORS AND TRAITORS

"The flower sheds its petals at my touch..."
—BÉCQUER

ANYONE who has had many years of successful experience with translation will be well aware that this type of work is, perhaps—and, at the risk of exaggerating, not even perhaps—of all tasks essayed by the inquisitive human mind, if not the most difficult, then certainly the least easy. *Traduttore traditore*, as it is said, obscurely, in Italian. Indeed, nothing could be clearer—but to what end? We shall here sketch out our own theory, in the logical order most appropriate to it.

First of all—and this is inherent in the well-known human condition—for treason to be treason it must not merely occur but also (to employ a commonplace) occur *consciously*, in various senses; second, the very fact of his undertaking the preparation of a new version of the text at all is a clear indication that the translator wouldn't dream of betraying his ward for anything in the world. It is something else altogether (and there are examples galore) when the translator is so careless that the betrayal is inadvertent or, as in certain cases, when he finds himself carried away by the enthusiasm generated by a genuine masterpiece. To summarize: Treason, as we have seen, must be *deliberate* in order to be considered such; and when it does occur, as frequently happens, it may be due to carelessness. And here we have the real problem, starkly divided into its two inseparable halves.

Only those who have never translated anything at all could possibly be unaware of the difficulties associated with translation. Let us see.

What should one opt for when one undertakes a translation: the letter or the spirit? This fresh dilemma (as though the previous one, outlined above, had already been resolved) weighs overwhelmingly on the conscience of every translator, in his private life. And with good reason. If, after agonizing over the matter in bed at night, he opts for a literal translation (which many advocate with a truly astonishing zeal), he will essentially limit himself to shifting words mechanically from one language to another (for example: the English *piano* = the Spanish *piano*; the German *Intellgenzia* = the Spanish *inteligencia*, etc.), thereby perhaps overlooking the cleverest idiomatic expressions and neglecting the excellencies of the former; or, alternatively, perverting the peculiar essence of the latter, in which *piano* possesses its own inimitable sound. If he chooses the second method, that is to say a more or less free translation, is he not essentially attributing the infelicities born of his own abject or mediocre soul to the sublime inspiration of his immortal author?

And so the most elementary logic might lead one to ask: Would it not be preferable to avoid translation entirely, at any cost? I certainly will not be the one to resolve this particular conundrum, which has been with us since Cervantes. For my part, I will merely remark that if, no matter which of these approaches it takes and from whatever angle one happens to regard it, a translation still seems bad, one should take caution and abstain. And indeed, abstention might be the only recourse available to us if the Stagirite had not unambiguously proposed that in such cases there exists an ingenious (as was everything he produced) solution, that of the middling path, or *aurea mediocritas*, as he rightly declared in due course, apropos of the no less unforgettable swine from Epicurus's herd.

This (so to speak) third position, or (bringing the metaphor to its logical conclusion) peaceful coexistence with a problem that is clearly insoluble from any point of view, does not sin by swinging the pendulum too far in one direction or the other, for in the end it can be reduced to a formula of mathematical simplicity: that one should employ a literal translation whenever it is possible to do so and thereby serve the spirit, and employ the "spiritual" or "free" translation whenever the letter demands it and theme, euphony, or events require.

Of course, the foregoing divagations would be inane if I myself had not lately dedicated a bit of my spare time to just such a divertimento. But now, to be brief—since time, as is its wont, is passing—I wish only to relate in a few words my experience translating a poem by the German poet Christian Morgenstern, especially since it represents a case perhaps unique in both languages.

Noting the poem's structure, I immediately found myself facing the famous dilemma: *letter or spirit*? And of course, in keeping with the line of conduct that I have traced again and again since childhood, I decided at last to opt for both, each in its own place. Here we have the original version:

Fisches Nachtgesang

and on the following page, on the extreme left and right, like the good and bad thieves in the legend, the *literal* and *spiritual* versions:

La Serenata del Pez
(The Fish's Serenade)

Nocturno en la Pecera
(Nocturne in the Fishbowl)

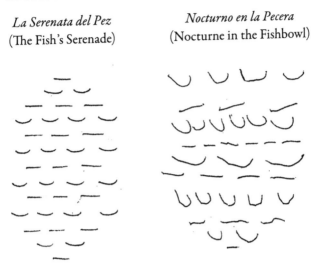

Now, to conclude—which of these two versions will the good or the bad reader settle on, since both of them exist? Unquestionably, the one that strikes each of them respectively as superior; or neither of them at all, if he exercises his prerogative of rejecting any work of art that is, by its very nature, subject to neither passions, rules, nor internal constraints.

THE BIRD AND THE ZITHER
(On a Forgotten Octave by Góngora)

TRADITIONALLY the poetry of Góngora has been viewed as a conundrum, one that presents the reader—even the most lay reader—with particular difficulties. Nevertheless, we are confident that said difficulties have been much exaggerated, insofar as the great majority of people fail to devote sufficient time to the thorough study of literary texts, particularly when said text is rife with hyperbaton (a difficult term to pluralize), or when insufficient attention has been paid to misprints. Nowadays we are continually hearing from the lips of some callow student or other that, for instance, *Ser y Tiempo* (*Sein und Zeit*), by the Teutonic philosopher Martin Heidegger, is a difficult book, which does no more than reveal a wholesale lack of attention on the part of the reader. What, then, will they make of Don Luis de Góngora y Argote (1561–1627), who took up his pen some three and a half centuries agone?

One of the more obscure octaves of his famous long poem *Polyphemus and Galatea*, included in his *Collected Works*, could be referred to, by means of antonomasia, as "the octave of the bird and the zither." In the interest of contributing to the elucidation of this fascinating work, and even at risk of being branded an imitator of other distinguished philologists and scholars, we propose in what follows to give our own modest version, as an homage, belated though it may be, to the fourth centenary of the bard's birth—everyone, after all, should do his part. For greater clarity, we will print two readings below, first that of the poet, and then our own, which are the same apart from a few slight variations; the accompanying scholia or commentaries will clarify what, without false modesty, we refer to as our own interpretation.

Templado pula en la maestra mano
el generoso pájaro su pluma,
o tan mudo en la alcándara que en vano
aun desmentir al cascabel presuma;
tascando haga el freno de oro cano
del caballo andaluz la ociosa espuma;
gima el lebrel en el cordón de seda,
y al cuerno al fin la cítara suceda.

Poised calmly, smoothing on his master's wrist
His feathers, let the noble hawk remain;
Or, silent on his perch, let him resist
The bell's injunction, urging him in vain;
Paling with idle foam his golden rein
Let the Andalusian charger champ his bit,
The greyhound whine to slip his silken tether,
And the song of the hunting horn succeed the zither.

Thus far Don Luis. And now, as they say, to take the bull by the horns:

Templado pule* en la maestra mano / Poised calmly, smoothing on his master's wrist

This presents no problems.

el generoso pájaro su pluma, / His feathers, let the noble hawk remain;

Is it here that the difficulties begin? As we shall see, they do not: the *"generoso pájaro"* is none other than the brooding poet himself[†]—

---

*"*Pula*" in the original version, an obvious misprint.
[†]Everyone is familiar with the comparison of the poet to a singing bird. Think only of Shakespeare, the "Swan" of Avon.

you will surely remember the image of Cervantes, immortalized by Gustave Durero, when he couldn't think of anything else with which to illustrate the prologue of his book—who, with his "mastering hand," "smooths," and for this we should understand "trims"; since in the most remote Antiquity, the feathers of birds were used to write, notably when poetry was concerned—his quill.

> *o tan mudo en la alcándara que en vano /* Or, silent on his
> perch, let him resist

This presents no problems.

> *aun desmentir al cascabel presuma; /* The bell's injunction,
> urging him in vain;

In Spanish symbology, the "*cascabel*," or "bell," represents happiness, and even merriment, states of emotion that the poet certainly doesn't feel capable of inhabiting at this particular moment (but be careful!: *only* at this moment; remember that Góngora was an Andalusian: see line six), mute as he is—that is to say, absorbed, and thinking of other things.

> *tascando haga el freno de oro cano /* Paling with idle foam
> his golden rein

This presents no problems. As with all of Góngora's verses—and this appears to have escaped the notice of the experts—it is immediately explained by the line that follows it.

Perhaps, to avoid misunderstandings, we should explain right away that "*oro cano*" (literally "pale gold") is none other than simple silver, and also point out that the "*h*" in "*haga*" should be aspirated, as if to say "*faga*," in order to round out the hendecasyllable.

> *del caballo andaluz la ociosa espuma; /* Let the Andalusian
> charger champ his bit,

"*Espuma*," "foam," is always "*ociosa*," that is, it is never still, especially not in the mouth of an Andalusian horse (as famous in its time for fieriness as Toledo steel was for strength) when it champs at its bit, not of gold, remember—there are no golden bits, or at least there shouldn't have been, at the time—but rather of silver, with which the mouths of horses were adorned in Andalusia.

> *gima el lebrel en el cordón de seda,* / The greyhound whine
>   to slip his silken tether,

This presents no problems. Hounds do indeed "*gima*," or "whine," a great deal when they are tied up with a silken cord. Here Góngora uses this familiar image to set off the effect of the magisterial hyperbaton with which he ends the octave under discussion:

> *y al cuerno al fin la cítara suceda.* / And the song of the
>   hunting horn succeed the zither.

The poet, in despair at being unable to think of anything despite the calm of his "perch" ("perch" = "chamber" = "study"), hurls away his pen (poeticism: "zither"), exclaiming:

> *Suceda al fin: Al cuerno la cítara!*

That is to say, "So what! To hell with the zither, let the chips fall where they may!" in a fit of rage so typical of the irritable character of Spaniards of that era—as it is of the race of poets in general, *genus irritabile vatum*, as Horace so snidely expressed it.

Reprinted from Revista de la Universidad de Mexico, *vol. XVI, no. 12, August 1962, reprinted from the Literary Supplement of* El Heraldo de San Blas, *San Blas, S.B., July 14th of the same year.*

A WRITER'S DECALOGUE

FIRST. When you have something to say, say it; when you don't, say that as well. Never stop writing.

Second. Never write for your contemporaries, much less, as many do, for your antecedents. Write for posterity, when you will undoubtedly be famous, for posterity is always just.

Third. Under no circumstances forget the celebrated dictum: When it comes to literature, nothing is written.

Fourth. Say what it's possible to say with a hundred words, with a hundred words; say what it's possible to say with a single word, with one. Never occupy the middle ground: That is, never write anything with fifty words.

Fifth. As strange as it may seem, writing is an art; to be a writer is to be an artist, like a trapeze artist or a wrestler par excellence—one who strives with language; for this struggle you must practice day and night.

Sixth. Make use of any disadvantages, such as insomnia, imprisonment, or poverty; the first made Baudelaire what he was, the second Pellico, and the third all of your writer friends; however, avoid nodding like Homer, or the tranquil life of a Byron, or earning as much as Bloy.

Seventh. Never pursue success. Success undid Cervantes, who was an excellent novelist until he published the *Quixote*. Though success is always inevitable, be sure to screw up from time to time regardless, so as to generate sympathy among your friends.

Eighth. Create for yourself an intelligent audience, which is easiest to do among the rich and powerful. Then you will never lack the sort of understanding and encouragement that flows from these two founts alone.

Ninth. Believe in yourself, but only up to a point; doubt yourself, but not too far. When in doubt, believe; when you believe, doubt. In this lies the only true wisdom that a writer can possess.

Tenth. Do your best to say things in such a way that the reader will always feel that, deep down, he is as intelligent as, or even more intelligent than, you. From time to time, he will be more intelligent than you are in earnest; but in order to convey this to him, you will need to be more intelligent than he is.

Eleventh. Never forget the feelings of your readers. Generally speaking, feelings are all they have; not like you, who lack them entirely, otherwise you would never have tried to get into this profession.

Twelfth. Once again, the reader. The better you write, the more readers you will have; as long as you continue to provide them with increasingly refined works, a growing number will long for your creations; but if you write with the masses in mind you will never be popular, and nobody will attempt to touch the hem of your garment in the street, or point at you in the supermarket.

Reprinted from La Cultura en México, *a supplement to* Siempre!, *no. 404, November 5, 1969. At the end of the introductory note to this and other texts by E.T. collected in this particular issue, one reads: "Finally, we must clarify that the* Decalogue, *according to our communications with Torres himself, includes twelve commandments so that all readers can choose the ten that suit them, discarding* two as they wish. 'Given that the human race has always rejected the Laws of God in their entirety,' he adds, 'this may be a somewhat naïve precaution.'"

INTERNATIONAL LIVING CREATURES' DAY

THIS MONTH the whole world will mark International Living Creatures' Day, which celebrates every living being in Creation, from the obdurate amoeba to the solitary conifer. It is said that the Kingdom of Nature contains one of everything; but within the Animal Kingdom one finds, if anything, an even greater abundance. Only pause for a moment and imagine a world *without* animals; it would be an empty world (though not one bereft of life, since there's more than enough of that in the Vegetable Kingdom), a world in which boredom would reign.

But aside from those of the mineral, vegetable, and animal, Nature contains one further kingdom, and a perpetually rich one at that: the Kingdom of Digression. Let us forbear from entering. The purpose of these lines is simply to guide the reader, as if by the hand (so to speak), into our little tribute to this holiday, which on the present occasion we have wished to render graphically—that is to say, without the aid of rhetorical flourishes or bothersome literary allusions—and in which one will find lions and wolves side by side, thereby providing a lesson to Man, who "is wolf to man," according to Hobbes—and indeed, from the wolf's point of view, "man to wolf."

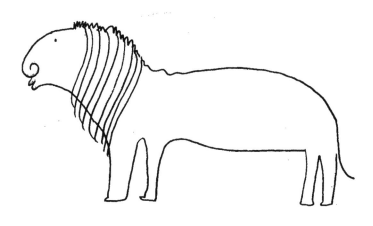

Lion

Phoenix

Wolf (pup)

Mosquito (1)

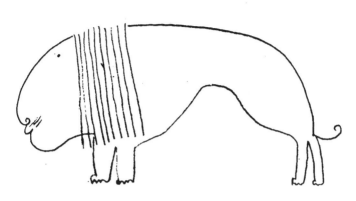

Lion

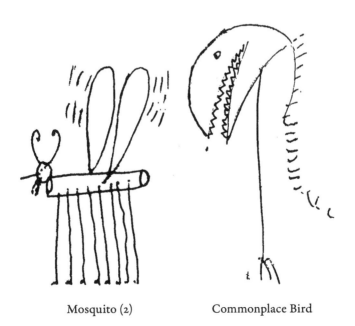

Mosquito (2)   Commonplace Bird

Reprinted from Revista de la Universidad de México, *vol. XVIII, no. 2, October 1963, which includes the following note: "On August 17, 1963, in honor of International Living Creatures' Day, the Literary Supplement of* El Heraldo de San Blas, *San Blas, S.B., published the drawings that appear below, accompanied by an introductory note by Eduardo Torres, the director of said supplement—a note that we reproduce here, though the opinions expressed therein remain the author's own."*

The drawings are reproduced here by permission of the aforementioned supplement.

Lions

THE QUALITATIVE LEAP

"Isn't there some species other than the human," she cried, hurling the newspaper down in disgust, "that one might be able to join?"

"And why not join the human?" he replied.

Reprinted from La Cultura en México, *a supplement to* Siempre!, *no. 404, November 5, 1969.*

AN ADDRESS BY DOCTOR EDUARDO TORRES TO THE CONTINENTAL CONGRESS OF WRITERS, HELD IN SAN BLAS, S.B., DURING THE MONTH OF MAY, 1967

IT IS HEREBY resolved:

(a) That better relations must be urgently established between male and female writers.

(b) That in order to guarantee in a real and effective manner the unhindered dissemination of their conceptions, from this day forward all writers of both sexes will be forbidden the excessive use of contraceptives of any sort, since it is widely acknowledged that numerous literary monstrosities of recent years (mainly in the fields of the novel, the short story, the essay, and the poem) have had their origins in that exotic practice.

(c) That to this end, ministers of education throughout the continent should be compelled, or advised, to read every book that they judge to be appropriate.

(d) That in the interest of allowing writers to suitably air their differences, fans should be situated ad hoc in the homes of the poorest, preferably in the vicinity of their typewriters or pens.

(e) That rather than persecuting male writers, the authorities should go after female writers—a task that, up until now, like a biblical curse, has been left entirely to the former, whose consequences the Department of Demographics (see their *Annual Report*, vol. 13, 1965), not to mention the less respectable medical clinics, are fully aware.

(f) That as an elementary courtesy, every book written by a female writer should be read before any book written by a male writer.

(g) That when publishing any sort of book, publishing houses should comply, motu proprio, with the preceding resolution.

(h) That when publishing any book of a subversive character, the publishers should throw a cocktail party for the authorities, so as to dampen the pernicious effects of its publication.

(i) That it is declared to have been sufficiently discussed and accepted that, among male and female writers alike, the right to a different opinion means war.

(j) That with the urgent goal of promoting relations between writers on this continent, it is declared obligatory that those who wish to be addressed as *tú* or as *vos*, be so addressed; that those who wish to be addressed as *usted*, likewise be addressed according to their preference; and that those who do not wish to be addressed at all should be addressed neither as *tú*, nor as *vos*, nor as *usted*, depending on the circumstances.

(k) That thanks to contemporary experience, it is recognized continent-wide that the best way of losing interest in the works of other authors consists of getting to know them personally.

(l) That ideas must be disseminated by way of whatever medium is available to their proprietors, the better to adequately deliver them to an increasingly large and ravenous public.

(m) That in order to defend themselves against the exploitation to which they are frequently subjected by publishers, writers, if they prefer to do so, should refuse to publish their books under the conditions laid out by the former, and take them instead to publishing houses that will be established by the state in accord with point (n).

(n) That it is recommended that the various states establish editorial houses (without in any way interfering thereafter with their day-to-day operations, of course) for the benefit of those authors who refuse to publish books under the iniquitous conditions imposed by private publishers, thereby preventing themselves from being bled dry by those with shameful intentions.

(ñ) That the state should provide, along with the usual lip service, housing for the best poets of each given year or month, in the location of their choosing.

(o) That in order to guarantee for our men and women of letters the repose that they so greatly deserve, it is recommended that they abstain, whenever they lack the requisite desire, from any and every variety of free love.

(p) That in order to eliminate the exploitation of their creations by the booksellers, all writers should send copies of their books, free of charge, to each of the members of this society, thus guaranteeing that the number of volumes they receive in return will multiply in geometrical progression (in accord with the growing number of members) for their solace and amusement.

(q) That when any colleague is duly incarcerated in any place whatsoever, whether for his political ideas, his vices, or his dirty tricks, all of the members of this society shall send him their books immediately, as a show either of solidarity or of frank repudiation.

(r) That we choose "To write is to live" as our motto.

(s) That given the vast distances involved and the increasing lack of time in which to read the works of our colleagues, we recognize the right of every individual simply to read his own works over again, at whatever length he deems necessary.

(t) That while the state is admittedly strong, when united we are even stronger than the state—for we cannot forget that as authors, male and female, our strength is, if not inferior, at least equal to that of the practitioners of any other art or science.

(u) That in the event of unjust imprisonment, each writer should become a veritable sphinx, producing enigmatic or unintelligible phrases whenever possible during interrogation, the better to confound the enemy.

(v) That when any writer is subjected to unjust and involuntary exile he should transform it—the moment he leaves the airport or the boat, if possible—into a voluntary exile, thereby discrediting the spurious government, or dictatorship, that sent him packing.

(w) That continual pronouncements should be made against war, which fundamentally produces nothing but annoyance, if not destruction and death.

(x) That writers should maintain among themselves an abundant and entertaining correspondence so as not to lose those contacts so painstakingly established thanks to this and similar congresses.

(y) That any criticism of this or future congresses of a similar character should be accepted without affectation or any false bitterness, in accordance with the principles that unite us, which are better, generally speaking, than those that divide us.

(z) Lastly, it is declared that every writer has the inalienable right to cast aside any difficulty or obstacle and to become a "best seller," without the latter condition elevating him in any way over his peers, or granting his publisher any particular advantage.

Reprinted from La Cultura de México, *a supplement to* Siempre!, *no. 444, August 12, 1970, reprinted from the Literary Supplement of* El Heraldo de San Blas, *San Blas, S.B., June 19, 1967.*

OF ANIMALS AND MEN

"'Drink in peace,' the cunning crocodile said to him."
—SAMANIEGO

OVER THE last several months I have yielded, more for literary reasons than anything else, to the temptation of not writing about the book at hand*; but from time to time I reflected that it would be better to wait, at least, for the second edition, which has now happily reached my desk. So then, let us get to work—without any of the timidity or lack of rigor that generally comes with attending to the work of friends.

The sporadic author of various enjoyable essays and stories, but before this of only a single book consisting of thirteen of the latter —*Complete Works (and Other Stories)*—first published by the renowned Universidad Nacional Autónoma de México in 1959, Augusto Monterroso, the subject of these lines, has today offered us a new volume assembling forty texts that, as with Rilke and his famous *Duino Elegies*, were written in a fit of inspiration, although in the case of our author the duration of said fit was somewhere in the neighborhood of ten years, for between space and time in his work there exists the same gap as between time and space as in that of any contemporary writer concerned with the passage of the one or the location of the other.

Now, could this be taken as a reproach? Yes or no, as one wishes. But once more, we note that *chi va piano va lontano*, as that quintes-

*Augusto Monterroso, *The Black Sheep and Other Fables* (Mexico: Editorial Joaquín Moritz, 1969; 2nd edition, 1971).

sentially music-loving people puts it. Likewise, it is easy to see that the extended wait to which Monterroso has subjected us yet again is less the sign of some morbid urge to torment the reader by confronting him with nothingness (Kierkegaard) than evidence of the calm rhythm with which he works, *exprimant* (as they say in France) his texts mercilessly in order to extract from them that bitter sweetness typical of certain citrus fruits, with which our author drives the stinger of his satire into the most inveterate customs, or mores, so as to castigate them *ridendo* (Juvenal), which tactic has produced such excellent results in all ages that in the present era wicked customs are all but nonexistent, except among the utterly depraved and their like.

But let us not stray from our subject, which, it may be assumed, is an important one. We say that Monterroso proceeds *piano*,* but must add that this slowness is matched by the paucity of his production. Which means that not only does he make us wait but when he finally delivers, he does so in small quantities. And here a fine simile springs to mind. Have you ever observed an industrious ant attempting to bear on her shoulders a load out of all proportion to her strength? How she suffers, stumbling here and there, fidgeting and groaning and sweating, and sometimes falling into a gentle sleep, during which she loses herself in unguessable dreams before rising once more to take up her burden; how she agonizes over the distance still separating her from her goal, where perhaps—in fact, certainly—the boot of some fiendish peasant awaits her, or maybe some malevolent little boy from the village who lies in ambush with a stick in his hand and an unmistakable smile of innocence on his lips but in his eyes the cold glare of those whose only thought is the destruction of diligent individuals contributing with their tireless work to the betterment of Society. So it is with overly protracted texts, especially when it's a question of brief works, rather than novels ... to which it might be maliciously thought I was referring with my parable, perhaps because of the extended feelers, or antennae, of that long-suffering insect. Let each, then, bear the burden that his strength permits, and recall that

*Slowly.

in any case plowing a field has ever been a task that Ox and Fly may carry out jointly—as I note without thereby wishing, however, to trespass on the difficult terrain of our author.

Who reads fables nowadays? Who reads the spiteful La Fontaine, the wise Aesop, the prudent Phaedrus, Hartzenbusch, the lofty Count, the amusing Lizardi? Everyone, perhaps because so many authors have tried their hand at the genre, and it therefore has something of the flavor of fruit from someone else's hedge (Garcilaso). Doubtless this is precisely what lies at the origin of our restless author's interest in offering us this handful of apologues or exemplary tales that, as has already been emphasized by both the daily press and the literary magazines of the capital, will find equally fascinated readers among children (see the fable titled "The Origin of the Elders"), youths (see "David's Sling"), and the aged (see the remainder).

But I beg you to allow me to add one further point.

Fully convinced that human beings are worthless, and that dealing with them or their problems (the latter seemingly as insoluble as salt in water) is therefore bootless, the author of this singularly heterogeneous book has, though he risks coming off as a skeptic, chosen to seek refuge from Man in the vast world of animals and other, similarly undervalued mythological creatures, like someone spurning a golden coin whose face is worn down by the incessant traffic to which it has been subjected by human greed. Thus, at various moments our curious author (an inveterate traveler, even if he modestly declines to admit it) ventures into the *selva oscura** of an unnamed distant land. And how different from ours is the world he discovers and depicts for us in this work! In that jungle we find no sellers or buyers, nor do the concepts of "yours" and "mine" circulate among the lianas, as in the Age of Gold. On the contrary, though the deni-

---

*Disoriented perhaps by the memory of Dante, nonspecialist critics have persisted in seeing in this *"selva"* an allegory of the human mind with all of its intricate, winding paths; we would only add that the human heart (Pascal), however discredited it may be in our era, has claims to assert here as well.

zens of that jungle are still part of a consumer society, consumption there occurs naturally: The animals need only to stretch out their hands (as Cervantes would have wanted), or lie in wait and sharpen their hearing (as Beethoven would have wanted), or fix their gaze on their prey and not lose sight of it (as Homer would have wanted), in order to secure their daily, or nightly (according to the variable habits or customs of person and place), bread. There, the traditional majesty of the Lion is, in fact, a *genuine* majesty (see page 11 of the volume under review, and others), rather than the affected posturing of our various emperors or heads of state; and the Gorilla occupies without any performative show of belligerence his appointed place in society, a society that lives together according to Divine (and, perhaps for that very reason, logical) decree: There the Monkey imitates Man, rather than Man the Monkey, as is generally the case among us; there the Donkey is stricken with fear when he encounters art, or love (depending on one's interpretation), as is only natural, and which constitutes a fine lesson for all; and, finally, there the Frog is a frog, the Chameleon a chameleon, and (to bring this already almost infinite list to a conclusion) the Pig a pig, though with the chops of a poet. Now tell me: Which *selva* is worse? The author, renowned for his innumerable and variegated ambiguities, discreetly refrains from opining, but the reader is free to air his suspicions and decide where he stands— on the side of the "uppercase" or of the "lowercase" jungle—in order to somehow escape from this labyrinth, like the aforementioned Dante bidding farewell to the dismal Virgil at the gates of Paradise. Regardless of which jungle one finds oneself in, of course, caution is advised.

As we have written elsewhere, the Kingdom of Nature contains one of everything; but within the Animal Kingdom one finds, if anything, an even greater abundance.*

What remains to be said? In these uncertain times, everyone is free to doubt or to believe, to come to his own conclusions, or to those of others. *Asinus asinum fricat.*

---

* For further details, see "International Living Creatures' Day," page 80.

Reprinted from La Cultura en México, *a supplement to* Siempre!, *no. 512, December 1, 1971; originally published in the* Literary Supplement *of* El Heraldo de San Blas, *San Blas, S.B., on August 22, 1971.*

IMAGINATION AND DESTINY

ON A HOT summer evening a man stretches himself out to rest beneath a tree, gazing up at the sky; an apple falls upon his head; his imagination sparks; he goes home and writes "Ode to Eve."

On a hot summer evening a man stretches himself out to rest beneath a tree, gazing up at the sky; an apple falls upon his head; his imagination sparks; he goes home and establishes the law of universal gravitation.

On a hot summer evening a man stretches himself out to rest beneath a tree, gazing up at the sky; an apple falls upon his head; his imagination sparks; he observes that the tree is not, in fact, an apple tree but rather a holm oak, and discovers, hidden among the branches, a mischievous stripling from town who amuses himself by tossing apples at gentlemen who stretch themselves out to rest under trees, gazing up at the sky, on hot summer evenings.

The first was (or became, and remained forever after) the poet Sir James Calisher; the second was (or became, and remained forever after) the physicist Sir Isaac Newton; the third might have been (or might have become and remained forever after) the novelist Sir Arthur Conan Doyle, but in fact became (or had irremediably been, since the days of his youth) the current chief of police of San Blas, S.B.

PART III: APHORISMS, MAXIMS, ETC.

A BRIEF SELECTION OF APHORISMS, MAXIMS, DICTA, AND APOTHEGMS BY DOCTOR EDUARDO TORRES, CULLED BY DON JUAN MANUEL CARRASQUILLA (SCHOLAR) FROM TABLE TALK, DIARIES, NOTEBOOKS, CORRESPONDENCE, AND VARIOUS ARTICLES PUBLISHED IN THE SUNDAY SUPPLEMENT OF *EL HERALDO DE SAN BLAS*, SAN BLAS, S.B.

Eager to bring honey home,
The questing bee forsakes his comb.

ABSTINENCIA / Abstinence
Only teetotalers think drinking is any fun.
—Spoken in El Fenix cantina; undated

Fling the door wide
For the departing friend.

AMISTAD / Friendship
A single friend is worth more to you when you're flush than three are when you're destitute. When you're flush, your friend will remain by your side; in poverty, you'll lose all three.
—Spoken in El Fenix cantina to the bartender, A. R. Sosa

AMOR / Love
Love exists just as long as it still doesn't exist completely.
—Notebook, Monday

APLAUSO / Applause
Even the applause of the foolish pleases the wise.
—Diary

ARTE / Art
It is always difficult to speak about art. Yet sooner or later the writer, dilettante, or mere entertainer will be obliged—either for a known reason, or any other motive—to do so.
—Lecture: "Must the Artist Be of His Time, or Vice Versa?"

ARTISTA (1) / Artist (1)
The artist does not create, but collects; does not invent, but recalls; does not depict, but transforms.
—Lecture: "On Art Considered as a Beautiful Crime"

ARTISTA (2) / Artist (2)
The artist creates, from diversity, unity.
—Ibid.

ARTISTA Y SU TIEMPO, EL / The Artist and His Time
Who knows if those bison in the Caves of Altamira weren't painted by Men of Their Time?
—*El Heraldo*, "Should the Artist Belong to His Time, or Vice Versa?"

BIOGRAFÍA / Biography
In many respects the genre of biography is no less difficult than that of poetry. Since the age of Plutarch, no biographer—not even Diogenes Laërtius or our own Boswell—has been able to uncover lives comparable to those of the ancient Greek master. The contemporary zeal for perpetual motion, combined with the inherent ease of modern transportation, means that too often today various lives, be they those of extraordinary or of commonplace figures, not only touch each other but actually *cross*—when the entire beauty of parallel lines lies in the fact that they never meet at all.
—Letter to Edmundo Flores

BREVEDAD DE LA VIDA / Brevity of Life
If we were able to shorten time the way we have shortened distance, we would be able to abbreviate life, and thereby traverse it in far fewer years.
—In conversation with Guillermo Haro; undated

CALUMNIA / Slander
There is no slander worse than the truth—but, like a little breath of wind that gradually grows in strength, the foregoing statement itself is an eternal slander of the truth.
—*El Heraldo*, "Homage to Rossini"

CARNE Y ESPÍRITU / Flesh and Spirit
No question, the flesh is weak; but let's not be hypocritical: The spirit is weaker still.
—Spoken in El Fenix cantina, November 1960

CINE / Film
The surest sign that film is not an art is that it has no muse.
—Letters (sent separately) to José de la Colina and Emilio García Riera

COMUNISMO / Communism
Communism cannot prevail. If it were to prevail, that would mean capitalism would *cease* to prevail, just as capitalism spelled the end of feudalism, and the latter, as we all know, supplanted slavery, a stage of Humanity in which all men were slaves. On the other hand, though communism is correct when it comes to economics, it is unbearable, despite, or perhaps because of, the fact that it is founded on reason. Communism cannot prevail.
—Overheard and recorded by H. J. Contreras, metalworker

CONTINENTE Y CONTENIDO / Form and Content
One could say that Africa (that is, form), which was once the Dark Continent, is nowadays a continent in a state of eruption, one await-

ing only the spark, or the fuse, which will ignite its powder (that is, content).
—Message to the United Nations

CONTRADICCIÓN (PRINCIPIO DE) / Contradiction (Principle of)
If it were not for contradiction, contraries would cease (so to speak) to exist, and, incidentally, to contradict each other.
—*El Heraldo*, Open letter to Víctor Flores Olea

CONTRADICTIO IN ADJECTO / Contradiction in Terms
The Unfinished Symphony is Schubert's most accomplished work.
—Memo to José Antonio Alcaraz

CONVERSADOR PLANO / Plain Speaker
One who, in conversation, is prepared to give his life in defense of a truth already universally acknowledged.
—*El Heraldo*, "The Decline of Conversation"

CRISTIANISMO E IGLESIA / Christianity and Church
The ideas bequeathed to us by Christ are so fine that it was necessary to create the whole hierarchy of the church in order to oppose them.
—Letter to José Revueltas

CRÍTICA / Criticism
Any of us might encounter a man locked in deadly combat with a pair of snakes; but when Lessing found himself confronted (*horresco referens*!) by this terrible spectacle, his first impulse was not to rush to the aid of Laocoön, like any other mortal, but rather to return home and write one of the great works of literary criticism.
—*El Heraldo*, "Luis Cardoza y Aragón, Subjective and Objective"

When a bad year draws to an end
An even worse one may be approaching.

DIARIO / Diary
Maintaining a diary is a spiritual exercise and pleasure neither practiced nor enjoyed by those who fail to keep one. To jot down a thought "is a joy forever." If the thought isn't worth the trouble, you should it jot it down in a special diary for thoughts that aren't worth the trouble.
—Note to Elena Poniatowska

DIOS (1) / God (1)
If God did not exist, it would be necessary to invent him. Very well—and if he *did* exist?
—*El Heraldo*, "The Village Agnostics"

DIOS (2) / God (2)
Only the enemies of God know God.
—*El Heraldo*, "To Create and Not to Create"

EDUCACIÓN SUPERIOR / Higher Education
Education must be expanded upward. In our own system, the ideal thing would be to increase the years of secondary schooling to five, and to abolish primary school.
—Letter to Henrique González Casanova

ENANOS / Dwarfs
Dwarfs have a sort of sixth sense that allows them to recognize one another at first sight.
—Letter to José Durand

> The farther away the rooster,*
> The farther away the broth.

ESCRITOR, ¿NACE, ES, O SE HACE?, EL / The Writer—Is He Born, or Made?
No matter what they may say, writers are born, not made. It may be

---

* Synecdoche for *hen*.

that, in the final analysis, some of them never die; but going back to antiquity, it is rare to encounter one that hasn't been born.
—*El Heraldo*, "Rubén Bonifaz Nuño y el Lacio"

ESTILO / Style
All literary works should be continually corrected and reduced. *Nulla dies sine linea*. Delete one line per day.
—*El Heraldo,* "The Physiology of Literary Taste"

EXPLOSIÓN DEMOGRÁFICA / Demographic Explosion
For whatever reason, the majority of Latin American nations are filled with children, adults, and the dead. As the first turn into the second, their state tends to worsen; in contrast to that of the second, which steadily improves as they transform themselves into the last.
—Note to Pablo González Casanova

FONDO Y FORMA / Form and Substance
No substance without form, no form without substance. Only when *both* are abolished can substance and form begin to exist.
—Letter to Salvador Elizondo

FRAGMENTOS (1) / Fragments (1)
Sometimes a fragment may be more thoughtful than an entire modern book. In its zeal for synthesis, Antiquity greatly cultivated the fragment. The ancient author who wrote the best fragments—whether with great discipline or simply because he was naturally disposed to the form—was Heraclitus. It is said that every night, before stretching himself out to sleep, he would write down that evening's fragment. Some came out so small that they have since been lost.
—*El Heraldo*, "Nothing Is Lost" (see supra)

FRAGMENTOS (2) / Fragments (2)
Fragments, as I've said elsewhere, have been cultivated in every era; but it was in Antiquity that they most flourished. In Europe, in all

eras, the greatest fragments have been architectural and sculptural; and as regards our ancient indigenous cultures, in ceramics.
—Spoken in the San Blas, S.B., ceramics studio La Rosita de San Blas, and much later incorporated in the article "Nothing Is Lost" (see above)

GENIO / Genius
If there were no geniuses, Mankind would lack the greatest works that it possesses today.
—Letter to Manuel Quijano

GUERRA / War
If it hadn't been for the Second World War, the Allies would never have dreamed of winning it.
—*El Heraldo*, "Victory Does Not Bestow Rights"

HERACLITANA / Heracleitean
If the current is slow enough and you have a good bicycle or horse at your disposal, it is in fact possible to bathe twice (or even three times, depending on your hygienic needs) in the same river.
—Diary, as transcribed by Carlos Illescas

HISTORIA / History
History never halts. Day and night, it marches incessantly onward. To wish to put a stop to it would be to wish to put a stop to Geography. Between the two there exists the same relation as between time and space, and no matter what happens, neither of them will stand still.
—*El Heraldo*, "Note to Peter Schultze-Kraft, Fabulist"

HISTORIA Y PREHISTORIA / History and Prehistory
One could say that, before History, all was Prehistory.
—*El Heraldo*, "Eduardo Césarman and Entropy"

HOMOSEXUALISMO / Homosexuality
Certainly most men who are *not* homosexual miss out on a raft of
pleasures too great to enumerate here; but they are also spared a good
deal of bother.
—*El Heraldo*, "Freud and Group Analysis"

HONOR / Honor
All honor to every gentleman.
—From a speech for National Postal Worker's Day

IDEAS / Ideas
The best ideas seem fated to fall into the hands of the worst human
beings.
—Notepad, undated

IMAGINACIÓN (1) / Imagination (1)
The imagination is more fantastical than reality.
—Diary

IMAGINACIÓN (2) / Imagination (2)
To achieve with the imagination the appearance of reality, and with
reality the appearance of imagination.
—*El Heraldo*, "On Carlos Rincón"

INSPIRACIÓN / Inspiration
There are those who claim that it exists, and those who claim it does
not. Literary history, however—though it often maintains a hypocritical silence on this point—is well aware that deep in his heart
every writer of talent conceals some great hidden love that has inspired
the lion's share of his oeuvre, and that said oeuvre would lose all of
its character were that love to be exposed to his wife, or, as is more
common, to the public.
—*El Heraldo*, "Columbus—Inspiration or Adventurer?"

INTELIGENCIA (1) / Intelligence (1)
Like almost everything else, intelligence is undergoing a process of democratization, in that it is no longer the exclusive preserve of the poorer classes.
—*El Heraldo*, "The Hour of All"

INTELIGENCIA (2) / Intelligence (2)
Intelligence tends to engender the sort of foolishness that only foolishness could possibly correct.
—Spoken in El Fenix cantina, undated

JUICIO DE VALOR / Value Judgment
We tend to have a false conception of false conceptions, inasmuch as whenever a false conception ceases to be such, it becomes a true conception, thereby demonstrating the injustice committed by those who considered it false, and not simply as a conception free from any moralistic or religious interpretation (false or no).
—Letter to Luis Villoro

JUSTICIA / Justice
If justice and reason are on your side, try to get them to pass to the side of your enemy, who will then be in a position to persecute you with reason and justice, and will, naturally, fail.
—*El Heraldo*, "Catalina Sierra and History"

> In the earliest hours of the morning,
> Meditating in bed.

LEY / Law
It is strict.
—Notepad

LIBRO / Book
Poet, don't give your book away; destroy it yourself.
—*El Heraldo*, "Letter to a Young Poet"

LUCHA DE CLASES / Class Struggle
The Rich should love the Poor and the Poor should love the Rich, for otherwise all is Hate.
—Quoted from E. M. Izquierdo, a Guatemalan thinker of the mid-twentieth century, now forgotten

MAGIA DE LOS ESPEJOS / The Magic of Mirrors
Terror of poets, refuge of critics.
—Letter to Luis Guillermo Piazza

MEDICINA / Medicine
Medicine does not always heal; sooner or later, death is its logical conclusion.
El Heraldo, "Medicine and Longevity as Seen from My Belvedere"

MILAGRO (INCONVENIENTES DE UN POSIBLE) / Miracle (Drawbacks of a Possible)
If by a miracle (that will never actually occur) the poor of some nation were to be changed into the rich, then logically the rich would become the de jure majority, with the consequent danger to the poor that—fatality of History!—they might let their guard down and find themselves as defenseless as they were before, when they were the majority.
—*El Heraldo*, "When Logic Goes Out the Window"

MUERTE / Death
"Epicurus was right: death does not exist. Only living beings fear it."
—Letter to José Luis Martínez

MUERTE (LA LUCHA CONTRA) / Death (the Struggle Against)
The best way to avoid death has always been to try to remain alive for as long as possible, provided of course that you don't make an effort so strenuous as to undermine the original idea.
—*El Heraldo*, "On Two or Three Texts by Juan Rulfo"

MUJER / Woman
Woman is the most marvelous being in Creation; though still a source
of endless difficulties. (See illustration.)
—Note to Efraín Huerta

One who is overly perfumed
Will tend to overwhelm her friends.

NOSTALGIA / Nostalgia
It's just around the corner.
—*El Heraldo*, "On Otto-Raúl González"

NUBE / Cloud
The summer cloud is transient; and great passions are like summer clouds, or winter clouds, depending.
—*El Heraldo*, "Francisco Giner de los Ríos in Our Midst"

ODIO / Hate
Love justifies all; hate justifies love.
—Diary

PALANCA / Leverage
There's no lever worse than one incapable of moving anything.
—*El Heraldo*, "Political Physics"

PASADO Y FUTURO / Past and Future
To remember: "I could never agree with the aberrations of the hyperboloid as proposed by de Sitter, since, according to Weyl, in reality the Universe is not without mass."
—Diary

PASIÓN / Passion
See *NUBE* / Cloud

PESIMISMO / Pessimism
When one door opens, a hundred close.
—Diary

PLAGIO / Plagiarism
An inevitability. Detestable, certainly, but sometimes it must be endured, for despite the multitude of thoughts bequeathed to us by Plato, Nature is so stingy that some men (and women) have never been touched by a single idea, and are thus forced to misappropriate

those of strangers, which are themselves generally spurious (if, indeed, said strangers possess any ideas whatever).
—*El Heraldo*, "Eduardo Lizalde and the Tiger"

PLATITUDES / Platitudes
I know that my enemies claim I'm a flat writer; and it may be so. But I always remember this line by Alonso de Ercilla (*Araucana*, Canto IV): "How good is justice, and how important!"
—*El Heraldo*, "Ernesto Mejía Sánchez and His Obsession with the *Lucida Poma*"

POBREZA Y RIQUEZA / Poverty and Wealth
Between poverty and wealth, always choose the first: You'll obtain it with less labor, and the poor are happier than the rich; the former fear nothing, but the latter can't sleep, since the poor are always weighing on their minds.
—*El Heraldo,* "Brief Lecture on Lord Keynes"

POESÍA / Poetry
Our poetry—like our tennis, and certain aspects of our demographic growth—is, happily, a mature poetry (see following illustration) from which one may expect magnificent, if painful, births.
—Letter to José Emilio Pacheco

PROPRIO VALOR / Self-Worth
This article has no merit other than being the best that I have written on the subject.
—*El Heraldo*, "Message to Bernardo Giner de los Ríos"

PROTECCIÓN A LA POESÍA / Support for Poetry
The nation's system of subventions has allowed our poets the sort of victories that silence would never have been able to achieve.
—Note to Carlos Monsiváis

PÚBLICO / Audience
The audience is always inferior to the spectacle.
—*El Heraldo*, "Chaplin's Cane as Inalienable Symbol, According to Otaola"

PUERTAS / Doors
Sometimes they shut; and at other times they open.
—*El Heraldo*, "The *Omnibus* of Gabriel Zaid"

RELACIONES OBRERO–PATRONALES / Employer–Employee Relations
A living employee is better than a dead employer.
—Journal (adapted from Ecclesiastes)

RIDÍCULO / Ridiculous
Man isn't content to be the stupidest animal in all of creation; he has to allow himself the luxury of being the most ridiculous as well.
—*El Heraldo*, "Humor and Humorousness"

SABER QUE NO SE SABE NADA / Knowing That One Knows Nothing
Socrates said: "All I know is that I know nothing." In Antiquity, this earned him the reputation of being the most ignorant philosopher in existence, a reputation that has lasted until our own epoch. His

student Plato, cleverer by far, insinuated that, in fact, he had only *forgotten* everything.
—Letter to Maria Sten

> If the root goes unappreciated
> How much less the opened leaf?
> If they should close an ear to you
> Profit by the one that's open.

SUERTE / Luck
See *PUERTAS* / Doors

TRABAJO / Work
Any nation in which the children are working while the adults go unemployed is, let's be frank, wretchedly organized.
—Spoken in the Fénix Cantina, May Day

UNIR ESFUERZOS / Joining Forces
Here in San Blas, numerous politicians who are either merely stupid or merely corrupt are awaiting the moment they achieve power sufficient to unite these two qualities.
—*El Heraldo*, "Ripeness Is All"

UNIVERSUM / Universe
There are few things like the universe!
—Notepad (strolling through San Blas, 11 p.m.)

VIRGINIDAD (1) / Virginity (1)
The more you use it, the less it is lost.
—*El Heraldo*, "Our Nonrenewable Assets"

VIRGINIDAD (2) / Virginity (2)
You have to use it in order to lose it.
—*El Heraldo*, "The Oil Is Ours"

PART IV: IMPROMPTU COLLABORATIONS

THE BURRO OF SAN BLAS (OR, THERE'S ALWAYS A BIGGER ASS)

(A SONNET)

In the town of San Blas, not far away   1
there dwells a useless ass, they say.
Everyone thinks he's exceedingly quick
but nothing of worth ever falls from his lips.
They say he's possessed of a quicksilver brain   5
but nothing of substance has dropped from his pen.
When he's piqued, he'll go off on one of his tears
(but mostly just sniffs into others' affairs).
He launches his clever critiques far and near
but nobody wants his hot air around here.   10
Before he goes off and gives *us* a shellacking
he ought to look inward and see what he's lacking.
If anyone reading believes what's been said,
he's a much bigger burro for having thus read.   14

ANALYSIS OF THE POEM "THE BURRO OF SAN BLAS (OR, THERE'S ALWAYS A BIGGER ASS)"

*by Alirio Gutiérrez**

I HAVE been asked† to analyze this brief work, which has circulated surreptitiously among the general public and not a few specialists in San Blas for some time in the form of printed leaflets, and to which I will now try my best to do justice.

Of course I must begin by saying that I can in no way accept that this piece is a sonnet, as its subtitle insinuates. Certainly the fact of its having fourteen lines brings the aforementioned composition into the orbit of that genre, but it is also common knowledge that apart from the famous *sonetos con estrambote* (that is, with an extra line— and doubtless so called in order to rhyme with *Quixote*) immortalized by Cervantes, and the sonnet with thirteen lines that occurred to Rubén Darío at an inopportune moment (and I say "inopportune" because it almost certainly came to him very late in the evening, so late in fact that he couldn't complete it, as he should have); it is well known, I should point out, that sonnets, aside from the requisite fourteen lines, should have more syllables per line than are present here, either eleven (if they're standard) or fourteen (if they're in alexandrines), with their corresponding hemistichs, and above all a disposition of rhyme that differs from that presented in the poem above—not to mention the appropriate distribution of stresses, which can fall now on one syllable, now on another. For the sake of greater

---

*A carefully adopted pseudonym. Nowhere in any of the civil or religious registries of San Blas does there exist such a pairing of first name and surname.

†In fact the document printed here is an impromptu contribution of unknown provenance, received by the Joaquín Moritz publishing house shortly before the preparation of this volume was completed.

clarity, I present below the rhyme scheme of a well-crafted sonnet (in order to avoid confusion I have suppressed the initial words of each line, but the reader can easily supply them with the aid of a pen):

_____	*quererte* (to love you)
_____	*prometido* (promised)
_____	*temido* (dreaded)
_____	*ofenderte* (offend you)
_____	*verte* (see you)
_____	*escarnecido* (mocked)
_____	*herido* (wounded)
_____	*muerte* (death)
_____	*manera* (manner)
_____	*amara* (would love)
_____	*temiera* (would fear)
_____	*quiera* (love)
_____	*esperara* (would wait)
_____	*quisiera* (would love)

Analyzed thus, "The Burro of San Blas (Or, There's Always a Bigger Ass)" presents us right from the start with considerable ambiguity (that is, ambiguity in the modern sense, since the contemporary reader isn't prepared to accept just anyone's statements as fact without further ado; and as will become clear, such ambiguity permeates line after line of this little work), given that an audience, not always terribly attentive to such matters, and unexpectedly confronted with something that seems to present itself as a sonnet but does not actually deliver, will in its ignorance be unable to tell whether this state of affairs is intentional or unintentional, or vice versa. Insofar as the form of the work is concerned, we must content ourselves with pointing out that we are dealing with an absolutely novel sort of structure (for which the anonymous author should be congratulated), one heretofore unknown and as yet unclassified, comprising fourteen lines, the majority octosyllabic, set in rhyming couplets resembling the sort known as *gaita gallega*:

I danced so much with the priest's housekeeper
I danced so much that it gave me a fever

but in lines of eight syllables. We've already mentioned that a number of lines exceed these dimensions, but it wouldn't be right to reproach the author for this—he should be praised, rather, for having discovered a new form, over which he naturally has certain rights; after all, it isn't every day that something new (apart from some slanderous lie or other) is conceived in San Blas, and it's certainly possible that any such defects are in fact a means of disguising more securely the hand of the master who devised them.

Even if the form of a literary work—simply because it concerns the material portion, that is, the structure—is easy enough to pick apart, as we have demonstrated above, the content is far less tractable, and often remains so obscure that in order to unravel it one must possess the patience of Job, or of an archaeologist (just remember the difficulties presented by the poet Persius in his time, to go no further than that). Here, as far as the content is concerned, we can immediately see that we are faced with an epigram, a genre as fashionable today as it was with the ancients. And truly, what could be better if one's aim is to denounce sundry vices, persons, and places? Human nature is always the same; man never changes (contrary to what the progressives would have us believe they believe), and the mistakes that mankind makes today are precisely those (recalling Quevedo) that he made yesterday and the day before yesterday (it isn't by chance that we mentioned Persius; and we could doubtless add Juvenal and Martial, if it weren't that the space we have allowed ourselves for this brief commentary were not drawing inexorably, little by little, like so many other things, toward its close), which means that as a form the epigram is never out of date and, very much to the contrary, is a genus or species that is always at hand, and it is necessary only to have the requisite genius to retrieve it and confer upon it once again its role as the mirror in which literature contemplates its own image, laying itself bare, and more often than not denigrating itself in an attempt to return to the Word its concrete significance, or bring it closer to the Thing in Itself, provided of course that the one who uses said Word takes note of it beforehand and strips it of the burden of supposed metaphorical senses that (poor oblivious creature) it has accumulated over time as a consequence of use, or better say abuse, which (as is always the case with abuse) results inevitably in degeneration, and exhaustion, as happens to commonplace metals in the alchemist's search for metal par excellence, which is to say gold in its pure state. And there we have the epigram: the pure verbal object stripped of all context, unalloyed, a return to the authentic, a cleareyed yet inadvertent tallying of the imperfections of a supposed other who is, in fact, none other than the poet himself, self-derided to an infinity in which limitation has no limit and opens onto a play of mirrors wherein the dream of the other reflects reality better than reality itself, and in which reality is the best reflection of the dream of the dreamed that one dreams within a dream.

But let us return to our text. Specifically, to its title. What does the title do, after all, if not launch us immediately into the endless chain of beings and objects?: The Burro of San Blas (Or, There's Always a Bigger Ass).

This subtitle, "There's Always a Bigger Ass," indicates that we will never lack someone who excels us in whatever sphere it may be, that the world is without end or limit, that even the stupidest of men (for the sense of the title is precisely this) could at any time of day or night console himself with the certainty that, stupid as he may be, or feel, there is always somebody out there (and here we have a fantastic contrast to the famous wise man in Calderón de la Barca who always encountered someone even wiser than himself, no matter how poor he became) more foolish than he is. There's always somebody else. As for the exegesis of the poem's final twist, I beg my reader's patience.

Now: Permit me to be direct. I know that, if I have been asked to analyze this more or less anonymous little masterpiece of our local literature for a book dedicated to Eduardo Torres, it is because the existence of a whole series of premises has been admitted, to wit:

(a) that the subject of the epigram is Eduardo Torres

(b) that I know the author of the epigram

(c) that the author of the epigram is me

(d) that the author of the epigram is Eduardo Torres

(e) that the subject of the epigram is me

Again, the play of mirrors. How it pleases me to imagine the reader's bewilderment! But tell me: If the writer isn't permitted to gloat over the bewilderment of the reader, then over whose should he gloat? His own? Absurd.

In any of these instances—(a), (b), (c), (d), or (e)—any final clarification will remain forever beyond our ken, as with the authorship of Avellaneda's *Quixote* or, perhaps more pertinently, the problem of Buridan's ass. If, in an inexplicable fit of sincerity, I were to confess that I had indeed authored the epigram, I would be betraying myself, at which point the literary effect of anonymity would lose all of its charm. On the other hand, if in a moment of carelessness I were to affirm that Eduardo Torres had written it, I would be instilling in the (not necessarily unsuspecting) reader the idea that its author was Eduardo Torres. Now, I don't flatly deny this, but given the doubt involved I prefer to lean toward the working hypothesis that the epigram could be from the hand of yet another party, as likely yours as mine, even if the twist in the final two lines is so much in the style of Professor Torres, so wholly in line with his type of conceptual game, that I do not rule out the possibility of his authorship, though this would make Professor Torres the only epigrammatist in the history of literature so wholly devoted to self-mockery. Anonymous self-mockery, I mean—make no mistake: Various others have denounced themselves, but always making sure to apply their signature before or after the epigram, which is much less serious, since by this means they secure for themselves the recognition of posterity, as in the case of Catullus.

Before accepting or rejecting points (a), (b), (c), (d), or (e), we will analyze the constituent parts of the text (all fourteen of them), in hopes that the effort will shed a certain amount of light on the afore-mentioned premises.

Line number one, "In the town of San Blas, not far away," is self-evidently false. Nowhere in the vicinity of San Blas would it be possible for someone to publish a sonnet in pamphlet form, due to the wholesale lack of local printing presses. We may establish thus that the author is not a resident of San Blas; this is a move no doubt intended to misdirect the reader's attention once and for all, though it is left to his perspicacity to perceive the sly wink that immediately betrays the satirical intent of the work.

Line two: "there dwells a useless ass, they say"—that is, someone extremely ignorant, or dim, lives in the aforesaid place.

Line three: "Everyone thinks he's exceedingly quick." This all but brutal swerve stuns the reader with its brusqueness, a brusqueness quickly and conveniently attenuated by the gentle melody of

Line four: "but nothing of worth ever falls from his lips."

Line five: "They say he's possessed of a quicksilver brain." One will have noticed that between the previous two lines (whose ingenuousness cannot be taken at face value) and the twelfth, the anonymous author fires off a barrage of rapid and overwhelming propositions and counter-propositions that again and again assail the mind of the reader, who is continually uncertain whether he actually understands what he's reading, bewildered as he is by these perpetual alterations, which are accented by the deliberate repetition of the word "but," that disjunctive conjunction that could—in an insincere show of lexical richness—have been replaced at least twice, once with a simple "moreover," and the other with a vulgar but surely no less effective "however."

Line six: "but nothing of substance has dropped from his pen." From the suggestion that the burro is a writer it has been deduced that the object of the satire here is Professor Torres; but so many people around here write (or *think* that they write) that the reference could be to any of the residents of San Blas, not to mention its surroundings. No, gentlemen: I'm afraid that things aren't quite so simple.

Line seven: "When he's piqued, he'll go off on one of his tears."

This is the critical point, the point where suspicion begins to bloom that the personage alluded to is indeed none other than Dr. Torres, since his natural propensity to attack at the slightest provocation from various bad actors in San Blas—whether rightly or wrongly, either in defense of the highest values or simply because he happens to be so inclined—is common knowledge, and has earned him both the antipathy and the almost unanimous sympathy of the majority of that city's residents, none of them terribly fond of being criticized (but fond, certainly, of seeing others criticized), be it for their habits or their actions. Hence the counterattack (immoderate, perhaps, but timely) of

Line eight: "(but mostly just sniffs into others' affairs)."

Line nine: "He launches his clever critiques far and near." As we can see, the satire's author is perfectly willing to accept *wholesome* and *constructive* criticism; what he will by no means countenance is criticism that is sly, disingenuous, faithless, or insolent; moreover, that particular sin is its own punishment, for according to

Line ten: "but nobody wants his hot air around here," this constant, gratuitous criticism, just or unjust, has lost all of its venom, since the locals, wrapped as they are in the cloak of habitual indifference, have been immunized against it. It is perhaps precisely on their behalf that the anonymous poet means to speak in the righteous couplet comprised by

Line eleven: "Before he goes off and gives *us* a shellacking," and, immediately following,

Line twelve: "he ought to look inward and see what he's lacking," so overwhelming on its face.

It is a truth commonly accepted that every beginning will have, sooner or later, the ending appropriate to it. Thus we arrive at the work's culminating moment, where the explosion of perplexity and astonishment can no longer be contained, for the reader has scarcely finished his gloating and let slip a satisfied laugh (like any other vulgar human) at the derision here trained on a figure as respectable (since even with all of his defects, what human being doesn't possess the same kind of flaws to a superlative degree?) as Professor Torres, when he finds himself blindsided by the revelation that the satire is aimed at none other than himself, the reader, who has been led through the poem as if by the hand only to see himself in this mirror, and whose face, in the wake of that first laugh, convulsive though it may be, will now fall in shame, if he indeed possesses any, at his own narrow-mindedness:

Lines thirteen and fourteen:

If anyone reading believes what's been said,
he's a much bigger burro for having thus read.

We have now examined various aspects of this little masterpiece, which has attained the status of a classic in San Blas. And yet, doubt persists, though we have some grounds now to venture answers to the famous five propositions:

(a) Indeed, it would seem that the epigram is (deceptively, given the ending) aimed at Eduardo Torres.

(b) I might, or might not, know the identity of the true or false author of the epigram, even though I choose not to mention it in the course of these remarks, whether out of modesty or because I consider it inappropriate to do so.

(c) The author of the epigram is probably *not* myself, first of all because of my natural respect for ideas, and then because deep down I feel that I would be incapable of achieving such heights (and perhaps also due to a misconceived humility).

(d) Given the overall mastery of the work and the wholly ingenious final twist whereby the reader is confronted with his own countenance, a technique dear to Professor Torres and one that has made him famous, the epigram could well have been written by him, employing a feigned self-denigration during the first twelve lines, and a brilliant *counterattack* in the last two.

(e) That the target of the epigram is myself is automatically ruled out by the preceding points (a), (b), (c), and (d).

And thus have I fulfilled, with *currente* (or *ocurrente*) *calamo* the honorable task entrusted to me of analyzing this jewel of our literature.

ADDENDUM

A FINAL POINT
by Eduardo Torres

IT APPEARS that the compilation of writings and other aspects of my life so long heralded by its author will at last be brought before the public eye.

Thanks to the ethical sensibilities of its director, Sr. Joaquín Díez-Canedo, the Joaquín Mortiz publishing house has seen fit to submit the final proofs of said book to my judgment, and to request my authorization for its publication—to forestall any future legal action or the like, one supposes.

Well, aside from two or three points that I'll touch upon momentarily, the truth is that there's nothing to object to, in terms of the editing. Yes, there are errors, for instance a few poorly transcribed sentences, including a handful that wind up acquiring a sense contrary to that which I'd intended, and several allusions to local political issues that I would have preferred to let go unmentioned. But few public figures are free from such things.

As for the book's author, I am aware—since I've known him for years—that he enjoys a certain reputation as a satirist, a reputation for which (forgive me) I don't particularly care. I first made his acquaintance when he asked my permission to reproduce the brief note on *Don Quixote* included in this volume in *Revista de la Universidad de México*—which permission I initially denied him, since I was well aware of the article's methodological inadequacy (after all, it was a fragmentary extract from my postgraduate thesis, which had been conceived several years earlier and finally was published in San Blas when the opportune moment presented itself). However, moved at last by the sundry reasons he offered (mostly humanitarian), I finally gave in, and there it remains, as the reader can see for himself, stirring up the sort of controversies which were the furthest thing from my mind while I was drafting it. As for the essay on Góngora...well, I certainly don't intend to tell the story of each of these humble approaches to subjects already much better addressed by various other sages and Hispanists.

I prefer not to comment on the tributes by my friends and relations, which are at times lightly falsified or indiscreet, except to state that, however much some may suspect it in the future, I haven't altered a thing, except perhaps here and there where a misplaced comma required it.

And now, since I've been presented with an opportunity unique in the annals of this type of work, I will add a few final words of a personal nature. And they are as follows: When I first read this anthology, it seemed to me that my own life, and San Blas, and my relatives and friends and enemies, had been a sort of dream, and that these crumbs were all that remained of it. Sometimes, rereading myself, I paused, glanced from side to side, and wondered whether I'd actually written the things that have been included here, whether I'd actually thought the things that I said, or the things that it's said that I said.

But whether or not it was a dream, and though we find Prospero and Hamlet standing hand in hand in the epigraph to these pages—an epigraph surely meant to confuse from the very beginning (though it's certainly none of my doing) anyone ready to delve in good faith into my circumstances—never fear: Sooner or later, when everything's said and done, all of it will wind up in the trash. If someday somebody takes up that trash once again and from it fabricates a few new sheets of paper, I trust that the next time around said paper will be used for something less ambiguous, less falsely magnanimous, less futile.

INDEX OF NAMES

BIBLIOGRAPHY

Aulus Gellius, *Attic Nights*

Bacon, Francis, *Novum Organum*
Bergson, Henri, *Creative Evolution*
Boswell, James, *The Life of Samuel Johnson*
Brillat-Savarin, Jean Anthelme, *The Physiology of Taste*
Burton, Robert, *The Anatomy of Melancholy*

Cervantes, Miguel de, *The Travails of Persiles and Sigismunda*
Comte, Auguste, *Positive Philosophy*
Chesterfield, Lord, *Letters to His Son, Philip Stanhope*

Darwin, Charles, *On the Origin of Species*
Diogenes Laërtius, *Lives and Opinions of Eminent Philosophers*

Eckermann, J. P., *Conversations with Goethe*

Florus, Lucius Annaeus, *Gesta Romanorum*
Frazer, James George, *The Golden Bough*

Gibbon, Edward, *The History of the Decline and Fall of the Roman Empire*
Goethe, J. W., *Dichtung und Wahrheit*

Hobbes, Thomas, *Leviathan*

Lévi-Strauss, Claude, *The Origin of Table Manners*

Machiavelli, Niccolò, *The Prince*
Marcus Aurelius, *Meditations*
Montaigne, M. de, *Essays*
More, Thomas, *Utopia*

Pepys, Samuel, *Diary*
Pliny the Elder, *Natural History*
Plutarch, *Parallel Lives*

Quintilianus, Marcus Fabius, *Institutio Oratoria*

Rolland, Romain, *Life of Beethoven*
Rousseau, J.-J., *Émile* and *The Confessions*

Santayana, George, *The Realms of Being*
Saint Thomas, *Summa Theologiae*
Seneca, Lucius Annaeus, *Philosophical Works*

Titus Livius, *History of Rome*
Torres, Luis Jerónimo, *San Blas, S.B., and Its Environs*

ABBREVIATIONS USED IN THIS BOOK

aff., most affectionately
att., attentive

B.A., Bachelor of Arts

Dr., doctor

etc., etcetera

h.s., humble servant

Ibid., *ibidem*
IBM, International Business Machines

m., meridiem

n., note
no., number
Num., number

p., page
p.m., post meridiem

Sra., señora

u.d., undated

vol., volume

1st, first
2nd, second

TRANSLATOR'S NOTES

EPIGRAPH

3 *The Tempest*: Clearly an error—though Monterroso ultimately leaves the reader in some doubt about who exactly is responsible for this blunder.

EPITAPH

5 As Jorge Ruffinelli notes in his heroic critical edition of *Lo demás es silencio* (Madrid: Catedra, 1986), to which the present notes are greatly indebted, the book begins with an allusion to the conclusion of *Don Quixote*, whose final chapter contains an epitaph composed by the knight's friend Sansón Carrasco. For a first-time reader unclear as to the ontological status of Eduardo Torres (is he an *actual* provincial journalist? a fictional character? an authorial stand-in? and then, *within* the fiction of the Festschrift we're now reading, is he alive or dead?), the opening epitaph has the effect of further muddying waters already considerably muddied.

5 *Benito Cereno*: A reference to the eponymous captain from Herman Melville's 1855 story describing a revolt of enslaved Africans on a Spanish ship en route to the Americas, collected in *The Piazza Tales* (1856).

5 *San Blas*: Ruffinelli remarks that there are at least eight hundred municipalities in Latin America and Spain named for Saint Blaise, the animal-loving patron saint of throat ailments and wool carders, who was tortured to death with steel combs ca. AD 316. Torres's San Blas is situated in Mexico, the provincial capital of the (likewise fictional) state of San Blas. Judging from the text attributed to Torres's brother, Luis, it seems to be a city big enough to support an opera house, a soccer stadium, an airport, a bullring, at least one daily paper, and even a subway system of some sort.

PART I: TRIBUTES

A BRIEF MOMENT IN THE LIFE OF EDUARDO TORRES

9   *Lord Jim*: As above (Epitaph, *Benito Cereno* note), an allusion to the eponymous protagonist of Joseph Conrad's novel, published in 1900. In both cases, the reference seems to have no deeper significance (except perhaps as a lightly satirical jab at the hidebound, Anglophilic literary tastes of a certain strand of Mexico's provincial intelligentsia).

12   *Mutatis mutandis*: Latin, "taking the respective differences into account"; *castigat ridendo mores*: Latin, "he corrects customs by means of ridicule," from Horace.

13   *Cincinnatuses or Cocleses*: Lucius Quinctius Cincinnatus, Roman statesman (born ca. 519 BC), proverbial for his selflessness in service to the empire during times of crisis. According to (possibly apocryphal) tradition, he left his small farm when appointed dictator during a military emergency in 458 BC, triumphed over the armies of the Aequi and Sabines in only sixteen days, then renounced his position and "returned to his plow." Publius Horatius Cocles was a legendary Roman hero famed for his almost solitary defense of the Pons Sublicius, one of the earliest bridges spanning the Tiber, during the Etruscan siege of the capital in 508 BC (and for having lost an eye in the course of that battle). Viriathus was a Lusitanian chieftan who died in 139 BC opposing the expansion of the Roman Empire into the western regions of the Iberian peninsula.

13   *excluded middle*: The principal of the excluded middle, fundamental for logic and mathematics, states that any given proposition is either true or false, with no permissible middle ground.

13   *Porphyrian tree*: Porphyry of Tyre (ca. 234–ca. AD 305) was a Roman Neoplatonic philosopher who, among other accomplishments, wrote the *Introduction to Categories*, an influential text that elucidated Aristotle's system of classifications; transmitted to Europe at large via Boethius's translations, its effect on medieval philosophy (and taxonomy generally) was significant. The Porphyrian tree was a diagram used to illustrate those categories.

13   *Gordian knot*: A legendary knot, all but impossible to unpick, said to have been located in the city of Gordium, in Phrygia; it was thought that whoever was able to untie it would be destined to rule Asia. According to tradition, Alexander the Great sliced the knot in two with a

single swing of his sword—"cutting a Gordian knot" has come to mean solving a seemingly insoluble problem by unconventional (and generally forceful) means.

13 *razor of Occam*: William of Occam (or Ockham, ca. 1287–1347) was an English friar, philosopher, and theologian. Occam's razor (also known as the principle of parsimony) insists that problems should be explained by using the fewest assumptions possible. Often explicated by way of the phrase: "entities should not be multiplied unnecessarily."

13 *Dixi*: Latin, "I have spoken."

E. TORRES: A SINGULAR CASE

14 *cultural supplements*: During the latter half of the twentieth century in Spain and Latin America, the weekly special sections of major newspapers (and indeed, as in the case of *El Heraldo de San Blas*, smaller local papers as well) covering literature, art, and ideas came to supplant many of the older, independent literary magazines. Naturally, their editors generally had a bully pulpit from which to lecture the public on intellectual matters.

16 *Captain Pedro de Enciso . . . the pure Quipuhuaca style . . . García Diéguez de Paredes*: All of the conquistadors named by Luis Torres here are fictional, as is the pyramid beneath the hill of San Blas.

17 *on whose holy day it was established*: The Feast of Saint Blaise is celebrated on February 3rd.

17 *the example furnished by a Cervantes confronting the blank page of his prologue*: Luis Torres alludes to the prologue of the first part of *Don Quixote* (quoted below in Edith Grossman's majestic translation):

> I wanted only to offer it to you plain and bare, unadorned by a prologue or the endless catalogue of sonnets, epigrams, and laudatory poems that are usually placed at the beginning of books. For I can tell you that although it cost me some effort to compose, none seemed greater than creating the preface you are now reading. I picked up my pen many times to write it, and many times I put it down again because I did not know what to write; and once, when I was baffled, with the paper in front of me, my pen behind my ear, my elbow propped on the writing table, and my cheek resting in my hand, pondering what I would say, a friend of mine, a man who is witty and wise, unexpectedly came

in and seeing me so perplexed asked the reason, and I hid nothing from him and said I was thinking about the prologue I had to write for the history of Don Quixote, and the problem was that I did not want to write it yet did not want to bring to light the deeds of so noble a knight without one.

17 *in vino veritas*: Latin, roughly "one speaks freely when in one's cups."

18 *the two cultures*: An allusion to novelist and scientist C. P. Snow's book *The Two Cultures and the Scientific Revolution*, which reprinted an expanded version of a lecture delivered at Cambridge University in 1956. In it, Snow argued that the separation of the fields of the humanities and the "hard" sciences by the British educational system, and their consequent estrangement from each other, had been disastrous for the development of both strands of culture and for society in general.

18 *ab ovo*: Literally "from the egg"; metaphorically, "right from the beginning." The tag has its origin in Horace's *Ars Poetica* (l. 147), where it is used in reference to Helen of Troy, born from an egg laid by Leda, who was seduced (or raped) by Zeus in the form of a swan.

19 *wool carders though they were*: Wool carding is the process of disentangling raw wool fibers in preparation for further processing; a repetitive and poorly paid job, it was conducted by menial laborers using metal combs well into the twentieth century, in areas where industrial means were unavailable. Though the evidence is still debated, it has been claimed that Christopher Columbus's father was a wool carder; and, of course, Blaise was the profession's patron saint.

19 *dura lex, sed lex*. Latin, "the law is hard, but it is the law."

MEMORIES OF MY LIFE WITH A GREAT MAN

22 *Bárbara Jacobs*: Jacobs (b. 1947) is a prolific contemporary Mexican novelist, poet, essayist, and translator; she was Monterroso's third and final spouse (1971–2003).

22 Epigraph: Jean-Jacques Rousseau, from the third volume of *Émile, or On Education* (1762).

23 *valet or not*: An allusion to the celebrated dictum of Louis II de Bourbon, Prince of Condé (1621–1686): "No man is a hero to his valet."

25 *a wooded and rocky landscape*: The allusion is to Leonardo da Vinci's *Mona Lisa*.

28 *the fatal thrust of the Duc de Nevers*: Philippe Jules Mancini, 8th

Duke of Nevers (1641–1707) was appointed as head of the king's musketeers when that military unit, formally attached to the royal household,
was reestablished during the reign of Louis XIV—they would later be
immortalized in the 1844 novel by Alexandre Dumas, père. A feared
swordsman, the duke was famed for his signature "Nevers thrust,"
fiendishly difficult to parry, which aimed for the opponent's forehead.

32 *Porthos*: The nom de guerre of the Baron du Vallon de Bracieux de
Pierrefonds, one of the eponymous musketeers (along with Athos and
Aramis) in *The Three Musketeers* by Alexandre Dumas, père.

36 *Incipit Vita Nova*: Latin, "here a new life begins." Dante begins his
book *Vita Nuova*—a pioneering work of poetry, autobiography, and literary criticism which broke with literary convention in utilizing de-
motic Tuscan rather than Latin—by identifying this phrase as a heading
from his "Book of Memory," his notebook. In Mark Musa's translation
(Bloomington, IN: Indiana University Press, 1973), the opening runs:
"In my Book of Memory, in the early part where there is little to be read,
there comes a chapter with the rubric: *Incipit vita nova*. It is my inten-
tion to copy into this little book the words I find written under that
heading—if not all of them, at least the essence of their meaning."

Luciano Zamora's description of his courtship with Felicia makes
numerous allusions to Dante. The final sentence of this section, "But I
read no more that day, and fell into a deep sleep, even as a dead body falls,"
fuses a pair of Dantean phrases, this time from the *Inferno*, canto V:
"Quel giorno più non vi leggemmo avante" ("We read no more that day")
and *"E caddi come corpo morto cade"* ("and fell, even as a dead body falls").

IT'S ALWAYS HARD TO TALK ABOUT A HUSBAND

50 *Siddhartha*: A novel by the Nobel Prize–winning Swiss German
writer Hermann Hesse (1877–1962).

52 *toston*: In Mexico, a coin worth 50 centavos, or half a peso, first is-
sued following the monetary reform in 1905; though no longer minted,
they remain legal tender.

57 *Archimedes . . . Marat . . . Charlotte in Weimar*: Here, in the process
of contradicting Luis Torres's description of her husband's bathing habits, Carmen seems to be confusing the assassin of the revolutionary politician and journalist Jean-Paul Marat, Girondin sympathizer Charlotte
Corday, with Charlotte Kestner (née Buff), a youthful lover of Goethe
and the protagonist of Thomas Mann's 1939 novel *Lotte in Weimar*.

58 *he would give his life to ensure that others have the right to give their lives for their ideas*: A comic mangling of the Voltairean mot: "I may not agree with your ideas, but would give my life for your right to express them."

PART II: SELECTIONS FROM THE WORK OF EDUARDO TORRES

A NEW EDITION OF THE *QUIXOTE*

63 *castigat ridendo mores*: Latin, "he corrects customs by means of ridicule," here mistakenly attributed by Torres to the Roman satirist Juvenal, rather than to Horace.

64 *a man for whom combat was rest*: A reference to a popular ballad quoted by Don Quixote in part I, chapter II of Cervantes's novel: "my trappings are my weapons, / and combat is my rest" (trans. Edith Grossman).

65 *peccata minuta*: Latin, "unimportant errors."

TRANSLATORS AND TRAITORS

69 *Epigraph*: From a poem by the celebrated nineteenth-century Spanish poet and writer of stories Gustavo Adolfo Bécquer (1836–1870). In a free translation from 1908 by Jules Renard (no relation to the French author of *Nature Stories* and *Poil de Carotte*), it runs:

> My life is a desert;
> The flowers I touch
> Lose petals and wither.
> The mischief is such,
> As if in my pathway
> Some foe seeded evil,
> So that I might harvest
> The crop of the devil.

69 *Traduttore traditore*: Italian, "to translate is to betray."

70 *this particular conundrum, which has been with us since Cervantes*: A reference to Don Quixote's dialogue with the translator in *Don Quixote*, part II, chapter LXII.

70 *aurea mediocritas*: Latin, "the golden mean," or "middle path."

70 *swine from Epicurus's herd*: A reference to the *Epistles* of Horace, i.4: "*me pinguem et nitidum bene curata cute vises cum ridere voles, Epicuri de grege porcum.*" As translated by David Ferry: "When you want a good laugh, you'll find me here, in the pink, / A pig from Epicurus's sty, fat, sleek, well cared for."

71 *Christian Morgenstern*: Morgenstern (1871–1914) was a German satirical poet best known for his 1905 collection *Galgenlieder* (*The Gallows Songs*), which includes this famous instance of visual poetry.

THE BIRD AND THE ZITHER

73 *agone*: Here Torres uses a Spanish archaism, "*habrá*," rather than the modern "*hará*."

74 *"Pula" in the original version, an obvious misprint*: Once again, Torres is mistaking archaisms for errata.

75 *Gustave Durero*: Here Torres conflates the names of Gustave Doré (1832–1883), famed nineteenth-century French illustrator of *Don Quixote* and many other works, with that of early-modern German painter and printmaker Albrecht Dürer (1471–1528).

76 *genus irritabile vatum*: Latin, from Horace, *Epistles* ii.2: "the irritable race of poets."

A WRITER'S DECALOGUE

77 *Pellico*: Silvio Pellico (1789–1854) was an Italian writer and patriot, author of the memoir *My Prisons*, and a translator of Byron's *Manfred*.

77 *nodding like Homer*: A reference to Horace's famous line in *Ars Poetica*: "*qundoque bonus dormitat Homerus*" ("sometimes even the good Homer nods"). Proverbially, "even good writers make mistakes."

77 *the tranquil life of a Byron*: As is well known, the life of the English Romantic poet George Gordon, Lord Byron (1788–1824), was anything but tranquil.

77 *Bloy*: Léon Bloy (1846–1917), a French Catholic novelist and essayist, spent much of his life in poverty.

INTERNATIONAL LIVING CREATURES' DAY

80 *Hobbes*: Thomas Hobbes (1588–1679) was an English philosopher and the author of *Leviathan* (1651). Versions of the Latin tag "*Homo homini lupus*" ("man is wolf to man") have appeared in works by Plautus,

Seneca the Younger, and Erasmus, among others, before Hobbes employed it in his introduction to *De Cive* (*On the Citizen*) in 1642.

AN ADDRESS BY DOCTOR EDUARDO TORRES

87 *the right to a different opinion means war*: A variation on the apothegm attributed to Benito Juárez (1806–1872), the twenty-sixth president of Mexico: "Between individuals, as between nations, respect for the rights of others is peace."

87 *that those who wish to be addressed as tú or as vos, be so addressed; that those who wish to be addressed as usted, likewise*: In Central America and various other countries of South America, *vos* is frequently used in place of *tú* as a form of address between close friends and relations. For a fulsome contemporary discussion of the history of this practice, see Proyecto Lingüístico Quetzalteco de Español, "¿Vos sos de Guatemala?" translated by Kirsten Weld, in *The Guatemala Reader*, edited by Greg Grandin, Deborah T. Levenson, and Elizabeth Oglesby (Durham and London: Duke University Press, 2011).

OF ANIMALS AND MEN

90 *as with Rilke*: Austrian poet Rainer Maria Rilke (1875–1926) composed his *Duino Elegies* during a ten-day fit of inspiration at the Château de Muzot in Veyras, Switzerland, in 1922.

90 *chi va piano va lontano*: Italian, "He who goes slowly goes far"; more or less equivalent to "Slow and steady wins the race."

91 *Juvenal*: Again, a misattribution.

92 *the spiteful La Fontaine, the wise Aesop, the prudent Phaedrus, Hartzenbusch, the lofty Count, the amusing Lizardi*: Here Torres rattles off a heterogeneous list of both well-known and somewhat obscure writers of fables. Aesop and La Fontaine need little introduction. Gaius Julius Phaedrus (ca. 15 BC–ca. AD 50) was a Roman writer of fables who also translated Aesop into Latin verse. Juan Eugenio Hartzenbusch Martínez (1806–1880) was a Spanish dramatist and translator who wrote several hundred fables in verse. "The lofty Count" is a reference to a collection of fables by Don Juan Manuel, Prince of Villena (1282–1348), titled *The Tales of Count Lucanor* (Torres seems to confuse the count, one of a pair of characters whose dialogues frame the fables, with the actual author of the book). Finally, José Joaquín Fernández de Lizardi (1776–1827) was a Mexican journalist and the author of what may be the

first novel to have been written in Latin America; his *Fables* were published in 1817.

92 *concepts of "yours" and "mine"*: A reference to the conversation between the goatherds on the subject of the Age of Gold in *Don Quixote*, part I, chapter XI.

93 *Asinus asinum fricat*: Latin, "An ass rubs up against an ass"; metaphorically, "idiots lavish praise on one another."

IMAGINATION AND DESTINY

95 *Sir James Calisher*: Neither poet nor ode have been found.

PART III: APHORISMS, MAXIMS, ETC.

100 *Diogenes Laërtius…Boswell*: Diogenes (180–240) was a third-century Greek biographer of philosophers; his *Lives and Opinions of Eminent Philosophers* focused on the intimate details of the lives of his subjects and was an important source for later writers. James Boswell, 9th Laird of Auchinleck (1740–1795), was a prolific Scottish lawyer, diarist, and biographer, most famously the author of *Life of Samuel Johnson* (1791).

100 *Edmundo Flores*: Edmundo Flores Fernández (1919–2003), a Mexican engineer, professor, and economist, was a friend of Monterroso.

101 *Guillermo Haro*: Guillermo Haro Barraza (1913–1988) was a Mexican astronomer and the husband of the writer Elena Poniatowska; the couple were friends of Monterroso.

101 *Rossini*: Gioachino Antonio Rossini (1792–1868) was an Italian composer of operas and chamber music, famous for (among many other works) *The Barber of Seville* and *William Tell*.

101 *José de la Colina*: Colina (1934–2019) was a Spanish-born journalist, essayist, and literary critic.

101 *Emilio García Riera*: García Riera (1931–2002) was a Spanish-born film critic, writer, and actor.

102 *Victor Flores Olea*: Flores Olea (1932–2020) was a Mexican professor and essayist, and a friend of Monterroso.

102 *José Antonio Alcaraz*: Alcazar (1938–2001) was a Mexican composer and actor known for his work on Alejandro Jodorowsky's *El Topo* (1970) and *The Holy Mountain* (1973).

102 *José Revueltas*: José Revueltas Sánchez (1914–1976) was a Mexican writer and political activist.

102 *Lessing*: Gotthold Ephraim Lessing (1729–1781) was a German playwright and literary critic, and the author of *Laocoön: An Essay on the Limits of Painting and Poetry*, a foundational work of eighteenth-century aesthetic theory, which uses a sculpture depicting the death of Laocoön in an attempt to delineate the distinctive spheres of poetry and the plastic arts. (Laocoön was a Trojan priest who, according to legend, was devoured along with his sons by a serpent sent by Athena to punish him for his attempt to warn Troy's defenders against taking in the Greeks' wooden horse.)

102 *horresco referens*: Latin, "I shudder to relate."

102 *Luis Cardoza y Aragón*: Cardoza y Aragón (1904–1992) was a Guatemalan poet, essayist, and diplomat.

103 *Elena Poniatowska*: Poniatowska (b. 1932) is a French-born Mexican journalist and writer whose *La noche de Tlatelolco* was a groundbreaking investigation of the brutal repression of student protesters in Mexico City in 1968.

103 *Henrique González Casanova*: González Casanova (1924–2004) was a Mexican professor, essayist, journalist, and translator, and a friend of Monterroso.

103 *José Durand Flórez*: Durand Flórez (1925–1990) was a Peruvian writer, folklorist, and historian.

104 *Rubén Bonifaz Nuño y el Lacio*: Bonifaz Nuño y el Lacio (1923–2013), a Mexican poet, classicist, and professor, was a friend of Monterroso.

104 *"The Physiology of Literary Taste"*: An allusion to the French lawyer and politician Jean Anthelme Brillat-Savarin's (1755–1826) *The Physiology of Taste* (1825).

104 *Nulla dies sina linea*: *Latin*, "Not a day without a line."

104 *Pablo González Casanova*: Pablo González Casanova y Valle (1922–2023) was a Mexican lawyer, sociologist, and historian, and the brother of Henrique González Casanova (see note to page 103, above).

104 *Salvador Elizondo*: Elizondo (1932–2006) was a Mexican novelist, poet, and essayist, whose influence on Latin American fiction in the 1960s and '70s might be compared to that of Alain Robbe-Grillet's in France.

105 *Carlos Illescas*: Carlos Illescas Hérnandez (1918–1998) was a Guatemalan poet, essayist, and screenwriter, resident in Mexico for much of his life, and a friend of Monterroso.

105 *Peter Schultze-Kraft*: Schultze-Kraft (b.1937) is a German translator and editor of Latin American literature.

105 *Eduardo Césarman*: Césarman (1931–2004) was a Chilean-born Mexican poet, essayist, and writer of novels.

106 *Carlos Rincón*: Rincón (1937–2018) was a Colombian critic, essayist, and translator, who notably brought Monterroso's volume of fables, *The Black Egg*, into German.

107 *Luis Villoro*: Luis Villoro Toranzo (1922–2014) was a Spanish-born Mexican philosopher, professor, and diplomat.

107 *Catalina Sierra*: Catalina Sierra Casasús (1916–1996) was an editor, essayist, and historian, and a member of Monterroso's literary circle.

108 *E. M. Izquierdo*: It is unknown whether Izquierdo was an actual Guatemalan literary figure—but given the conjunction of this entry's title and the Spanish meaning of *izquierdo* ("left"), the name's appearance here is almost certainly a joke.

108 *Luis Guillermo Piazza*: Luis Guillermo Piazza Rennella (1921–2007) was an Argentine-born writer of essays, novels, and poems; a co-founder of the publishing house Editorial Novaro; and part of Monterroso's literary circle.

108 *José Luis Martínez*: Martínez (1918–2007) was a Mexican literary critic and essayist.

108 *Juan Rulfo*: Juan Nepomuceno Carlos Pérez Rulfo Vizcaíno (1917–1986) was an enormously influential Mexican novelist, screenwriter, and photographer, and a close friend, confidant, and occasional literary rival of Monterroso. Rulfo published only three books during his lifetime—one of which, *Pedro Páramo*, is a slim late-modernist masterpiece that has acquired a reputation as one of the most important novels written in Mexico.

110 *Otto-Raúl González*: González (1921–2007) was a prolific Guatemalan poet and critic, a member of the "Generation of '40," and served as undersecretary of the country's land reform program under the Arbenz government. In the wake of the 1954 coup d'état he was forced to flee, and lived the rest of his life in Mexico, where he was a close friend of Monterroso.

110 *Francisco Giner de los Ríos*: Giner de los Ríos (1839–1915) was a Spanish philosopher, essayist, and educator; one of his major contributions to the development of Spanish (and by extension, Latin American)

culture was his 1876 founding of the independent Institución Libre de Enseñanza (Institute for Free Education), following the expulsion from Madrid's Central University of a number of professors who had opposed the government's (and the church's) veto power over curricula. The list of intellectuals and artists associated with the Institute as either instructors or scholars represents a who's who of Spanish intellectual life in the late nineteenth and early twentieth centuries.

110 *de Sitter...Weyl*: Willem de Sitter (1872–1934) was a Dutch mathematician, astronomer, cosmologist, and professor, who collaborated with Albert Einstein and was an important commentator on his work. Hermann Weyl (1885–1955) was a German mathematician who made significant contributions to the field of theoretical physics, specifically general relativity.

111 *Eduardo Lizalde*: Eduardo Lizalde Chávez (1929–2022) was a Mexican poet and professor, and part of Monterroso's literary circle.

111 *Ernesto Mejía Sánchez*: Mejía Sánchez (1923–1985) was a Nicaraguan poet, story writer, and critic.

111 *Lord Keynes*: John Maynard Keynes, 1st Baron Keynes (1883–1946) was a profoundly influential English economist and philosopher who challenged the understandings of neoclassical economics.

111 *José Emilio Pacheco*: Pacheco (1939–2014), an influential Mexican poet, essayist, novelist, and writer of stories, was a close friend and collaborator of Monterroso (and published a highly comic "appreciation" of Eduardo Torres after the publication of *The Rest Is Silence*).

113 *Bernardo Giner de los Ríos*: Giner de los Ríos (1888–1970) was a Spanish-born architect and politician who served as Minister of Public Works for the Republican government in Spain during the Civil War; afterward he resided in Mexico for much of his life, where he wrote historical and theoretical works about Spanish architecture.

113 *Carlos Monsiváis*: Carlos Monsiváis Aceves (1938–2010) was a Mexican journalist, critic, and philosopher, and part of Monterroso's literary circle.

113 *Gabriel Zaid*: Zaid (b. 1934) is a Mexican poet and essayist.

113 *Ecclesiastes*: A reference to the famous line in Ecclesiastes 9:4: "For to him that is joined to all the living there is hope: for a living dog is better than a dead lion." (King James Version)

114 *Maria Sten*: Sten (1917–2007) was a Mexican Polish literary historian and translator.

PART IV: IMPROMPTU COLLABORATIONS

THE BURRO OF SAN BLAS

117   The original reads:

> *Aquí muy cerca, en San Blas*
> *vive un burro por demás.*
> *Todos piensan que es muy sabio*
> *pero nada bueno sale de su labio.*
> *Dicen que es de cerebro pronto*
> *pero lo que escribe siempre es tonto.*
> *Contra cualquiera arremete*
> *metiéndose en lo que no le compete.*
> *Critica a todos con maña*
> *pero aquí ya a nadie engaña.*
> *Antes que a otros criticar*
> *sus defectos debería mirar.*
> *Si el que lee esto se lo cree*
> *es más tonto que él, puesto que lo lee.*

ANALYSIS OF THE POEM "THE BURRO OF SAN BLAS"

118   *Rubén Darío*: Félix Rubén García Sarmiento (1867–1916) was a Nicaraguan poet who inaugurated the late nineteenth-century modernist movement in Spanish-language literature.

119   *the rhyme scheme of a well-crafted sonnet*: The poem in question is "Sonnet to Christ Crucified," a famous anonymous composition first published in Spain in 1628, and attributed over the years (with little foundation) to various authors including Saint Teresa of Avila, Lope de Vega, and others. It begins with the lines: *"No me mueve mi Dios para quererte / el Cielo que me tienes prometido."* ("What moves me to love you, my Lord, is not / the heaven that you have promised me.")

119   *gaita gallega*: The Galician gaita is a traditional Galician and Portuguese instrument, a kind of bagpipe, which has given its name to the metrical form of popular songs sung to its music.

120   *I danced so much…it gave me a fever*: *"tanto bailé con el ama del cura / tanto bailé que me dio calenture."*

120   *epigram*: Traditionally, a short, often satirical poem.

121 *the famous wise man in Calderón de la Barca*: An allusion to the ten-
line anecdote in Calderón de la Barca's Golden Age play, *Life Is a Dream*:

> *Cuentan de un sabio que un día*
> *tan pobre y mísero estaba,*
> *que sólo se sustentaba*
> *de unas hierbas que cogía.*
> *¿Habrá otro, entre sí decía,*
>
> *más pobre y triste que yo?;*
> *y cuando el rostro volvió*
> *halló la respuesta, viendo*
> *que otro sabio iba cogiendo*
> *las hierbas que él arrojó.*

> They tell of a wise man who one day
> found himself so poor and miserable
> that a handful of weeds plucked from the earth
> were all that kept him fed.
> Will there ever be another, he asked himself,
>
> sadder and poorer than I?;
> and turning his head
> found the answer, seeing
> another wise man collecting the herbs
> that he had rejected.

122 *Avellaneda's Quixote*: Alonso Fernández de Avellaneda was the
pseudonym of a Peninsular author who published a sequel to *Don Quixote* in 1614, before Cervantes was able to complete and print his own
second volume. His true identity remains unknown. Cervantes himself
makes metafictional hay of the existence of Avellaneda's text in the latter half of his book, when Don Quixote finds himself encountering
people who have read the apocryphal *Quixote*—and indeed, at least one
character who actually *originates* in Avellaneda's knockoff. In his prose
piece "On Attributions," from *Perpetual Motion*, Monterroso specu-
lates that "Avellaneda" may in fact have been Cervantes himself.

122 *Buridan's ass*: Jean Buridan (1301–1358) was a French philosopher

and professor at the University of Paris. According to the *Oxford Dictionary of Phrase and Fable*, Buridan's ass is a philosophical paradox in which "a hungry and thirsty donkey, placed between a bundle of hay and a pail of water, would die of hunger and thirst because there was no reason for him to choose one resource over the other."

125 *currente calamo*: Latin, literally "with running pen," metaphorically "offhand, without much forethought." Here Torres puns with the Spanish *ocurrente*: "witty or clever."

ADDENDUM

A FINAL POINT

129 *Joaquín Díez-Canedo*: Díez-Canedo (b. 1955) is a Mexican editor and translator. He was the director of the Joaquín Moritz publishing house when it first released *The Rest Is Silence* in 1978; from 2009 until 2013, he was the director of Mexico's Fondo de Cultura Económica, a vastly important, nonprofit publisher financially supported by the Mexican government.

OTHER NEW YORK REVIEW CLASSICS

For a complete list of titles, visit www.nyrb.com.

ADOLFO BIOY CASARES The Invention of Morel

ROBERT MONTGOMERY BIRD Sheppard Lee, Written by Himself

PAUL BLACKBURN (TRANSLATOR) Proensa

CAROLINE BLACKWOOD Corrigan

CAROLINE BLACKWOOD Great Granny Webster

LESLEY BLANCH Journey into the Mind's Eye: Fragments of an Autobiography

RONALD BLYTHE Akenfield: Portrait of an English Village

HENRI BOSCO The Child and the River

HENRI BOSCO Malicroix

NICOLAS BOUVIER The Way of the World

EMMANUEL BOVE Henri Duchemin and His Shadows

EMMANUEL BOVE My Friends

MALCOLM BRALY On the Yard

MILLEN BRAND The Outward Room

ROBERT BRESSON Notes on the Cinematograph

DAVID BROMWICH (EDITOR) Writing Politics: An Anthology

SIR THOMAS BROWNE Religio Medici and Urne-Buriall

DAVID R. BUNCH Moderan

JOHN HORNE BURNS The Gallery

ROBERT BURTON The Anatomy of Melancholy

DINO BUZZATI A Love Affair

DINO BUZZATI The Singularity

DINO BUZZATI The Stronghold

INÈS CAGNATI Free Day

MATEI CALINESCU The Life and Opinions of Zacharias Lichter

GIROLAMO CARDANO The Book of My Life

DON CARPENTER Hard Rain Falling

J.L. CARR A Month in the Country

LEONORA CARRINGTON Down Below

LEONORA CARRINGTON The Hearing Trumpet

CAMILO JOSÉ CELA The Hive

BLAISE CENDRARS Moravagine

EILEEN CHANG Little Reunions

EILEEN CHANG Love in a Fallen City

EILEEN CHANG Naked Earth

EILEEN CHANG Written on Water

JOAN CHASE During the Reign of the Queen of Persia

FRANÇOIS-RENÉ DE CHATEAUBRIAND Memoirs from Beyond the Grave, 1768–1800

FRANÇOIS-RENÉ DE CHATEAUBRIAND Memoirs from Beyond the Grave, 1800–1815

UPAMANYU CHATTERJEE English, August: An Indian Story

AMIT CHAUDHURI Afternoon Raag

AMIT CHAUDHURI Freedom Song

AMIT CHAUDHURI A Strange and Sublime Address

NIRAD C. CHAUDHURI The Autobiography of an Unknown Indian

ELLIOTT CHAZE Black Wings Has My Angel

ANTON CHEKHOV Peasants and Other Stories

GABRIEL CHEVALLIER Fear: A Novel of World War I

JEAN-PAUL CLÉBERT Paris Vagabond

LUCILLE CLIFTON Generations: A Memoir

RICHARD COBB Paris and Elsewhere

RACHEL COHEN A Chance Meeting: American Encounters

COLETTE Chéri *and* The End of Chéri

JOHN COLLIER Fancies and Goodnights

MAVIS GALLANT The Cost of Living: Early and Uncollected Stories
MAVIS GALLANT Paris Stories
MAVIS GALLANT Varieties of Exile
GABRIEL GARCÍA MÁRQUEZ Clandestine in Chile: The Adventures of Miguel Littín
LEONARD GARDNER Fat City
WILLIAM H. GASS In the Heart of the Heart of the Country and Other Stories
WILLIAM H. GASS On Being Blue: A Philosophical Inquiry
THÉOPHILE GAUTIER My Fantoms
GE FEI The Invisibility Cloak
GE FEI Peach Blossom Paradise
JEAN GENET The Criminal Child: Selected Essays
ANDRÉ GIDE Marshlands
ÉLISABETH GILLE The Mirador: Dreamed Memories of Irène Némirovsky by Her Daughter
FRANÇOISE GILOT Life with Picasso
NATALIA GINZBURG Family *and* Borghesia
NATALIA GINZBURG Family Lexicon
JEAN GIONO A King Alone
JEAN GIONO The Open Road
JOHN GLASSCO Memoirs of Montparnasse
P.V. GLOB The Bog People: Iron-Age Man Preserved
ROBERT GLÜCK Margery Kempe
NIKOLAI GOGOL Dead Souls
EDMOND AND JULES DE GONCOURT Pages from the Goncourt Journals
ALICE GOODMAN History Is Our Mother: Three Libretti
PAUL GOODMAN Growing Up Absurd: Problems of Youth in the Organized Society
EDWARD GOREY (EDITOR) The Haunted Looking Glass
JEREMIAS GOTTHELF The Black Spider
JULIEN GRACQ Balcony in the Forest
A.C. GRAHAM Poems of the Late T'ang
HENRY GREEN Nothing
HENRY GREEN Party Going
HENRY GREEN Surviving
WILLIAM LINDSAY GRESHAM Nightmare Alley
HANS HERBERT GRIMM Schlump
EMMETT GROGAN Ringolevio: A Life Played for Keeps
VASILY GROSSMAN Life and Fate
VASILY GROSSMAN The People Immortal
VASILY GROSSMAN Stalingrad
LOUIS GUILLOUX Blood Dark
OAKLEY HALL Warlock
PATRICK HAMILTON The Slaves of Solitude
PATRICK HAMILTON Twenty Thousand Streets Under the Sky
PETER HANDKE Short Letter, Long Farewell
PETER HANDKE Slow Homecoming
MARTIN A. HANSEN The Liar
THORKILD HANSEN Arabia Felix: The Danish Expedition of 1761–1767
ELIZABETH HARDWICK Seduction and Betrayal
ELIZABETH HARDWICK Sleepless Nights
ELIZABETH HARDWICK The Uncollected Essays of Elizabeth Hardwick
L.P. HARTLEY The Go-Between
NATHANIEL HAWTHORNE Twenty Days with Julian & Little Bunny by Papa
ALFRED HAYES The End of Me
ALFRED HAYES In Love

SILVINA OCAMPO Thus Were Their Faces

IONA AND PETER OPIE The Lore and Language of Schoolchildren

IRIS ORIGO A Chill in the Air: An Italian War Diary, 1939–1940

MAXIM OSIPOV Kilometer 101

MAXIM OSIPOV Rock, Paper, Scissors and Other Stories

IRIS OWENS After Claude

LEV OZEROV Portraits Without Frames

RUSSELL PAGE The Education of a Gardener

ALEXANDROS PAPADIAMANTIS The Murderess

PIER PAOLO PASOLINI Boys Alive

BORIS PASTERNAK, MARINA TSVETAYEVA, AND RAINER MARIA RILKE Letters, Summer 1926

KONSTANTIN PAUSTOVSKY The Story of a Life

CESARE PAVESE The Selected Works of Cesare Pavese

DOUGLAS J. PENICK The Oceans of Cruelty: Twenty-Five Tales of a Corpse-Spirit, a Retelling

ELEANOR PERÉNYI More Was Lost: A Memoir

LUIGI PIRANDELLO The Late Mattia Pascal

JOSEP PLA The Gray Notebook

DAVID PLANTE Difficult Women: A Memoir of Three

ANDREY PLATONOV Chevengur

NORMAN PODHORETZ Making It

J.F. POWERS The Stories of J.F. Powers

CHRISTOPHER PRIEST Inverted World

MARCEL PROUST Swann's Way

BOLESŁAW PRUS The Doll

GEORGE PSYCHOUNDAKIS The Cretan Runner: His Story of the German Occupation

ALEXANDER PUSHKIN Peter the Great's African: Experiments in Prose

QIU MIAOJIN Last Words from Montmartre

QIU MIAOJIN Notes of a Crocodile

RAYMOND QUENEAU The Skin of Dreams

PAUL RADIN Primitive Man as Philosopher

GRACILIANO RAMOS São Bernardo

FRIEDRICH RECK Diary of a Man in Despair

JULES RENARD Nature Stories

JEAN RENOIR Renoir, My Father

GREGOR VON REZZORI Memoirs of an Anti-Semite

JULIO RAMÓN RIBEYRO The Word of the Speechless: Selected Stories

TIM ROBINSON Stones of Aran: Labyrinth

MAXIME RODINSON Muḥammad

MILTON ROKEACH The Three Christs of Ypsilanti

FR. ROLFE Hadrian the Seventh

LINDA ROSENKRANTZ Talk

LILLIAN ROSS Picture

WILLIAM ROUGHEAD Classic Crimes

CONSTANCE ROURKE American Humor: A Study of the National Character

RUMI Gold; translated by Haleh Liza Gafori

UMBERTO SABA Ernesto

SAKI The Unrest-Cure and Other Stories; illustrated by Edward Gorey

JOAN SALES Uncertain Glory

TAYEB SALIH Season of Migration to the North

TAYEB SALIH The Wedding of Zein

FELIX SALTEN Bambi; or, Life in the Forest

JEAN-PAUL SARTRE We Have Only This Life to Live: Selected Essays. 1939–1975